All Or
NOTHING

All Or NOTHING

an Abbott Springs romance

LEXI RYAN

For Rhonda, who put the idea out there, and Marilyn and Caisey, who jumped on board.

CHAPTER
One

She should have been here. I stared at the empty wooden chair next to me, and it stared back. If furniture could talk, this rickety piece of shit was telling me I was an idiot.

Fucking fantastic. Now I wasn't just contemplating talking furniture, the talking furniture was smarter than me.

"Have you heard from Aubree?"

"What?" Maya's mention of my long-time best friend nearly had me jumping out of my skin. I should have expected her name to come up, but I hadn't fully prepared myself for it.

Maya narrowed her eyes at me like I was acting strange. Which I was. My friends and I met at Juke's Box every year to kick off Winterfest weekend. We had since we were teens, since Juke wasn't one to worry himself much about silly things like excise laws.

Instead of enjoying the company and the tradition, I couldn't stop obsessing over how wrong everything felt without Aubree Baxter.

"What time did she say her plane was landing?" Maya asked, rooting in her purse for her phone.

Across the table, Sami tapped at her phone. "She landed an hour ago." She bit back a laugh. "She said her dad sent a limo to pick her up."

"We could have done it," Maya said. "I hate that she's alone the whole drive from the airport."

"Right." Craig Walton drummed his fingers on the table. "A limo ride is so tough. She's probably sipping champagne as we speak. Poor Aubree."

Even though he'd gone to high school with us, Craig didn't really fit into our little group. He'd inserted himself into it over the last couple of years, hoping—best I could tell—to find his way into Bree's pants. If there was a God above, that would never happen.

My mind spun. Aubree. Here. Tonight.

The last time I'd seen Aubree, she'd been naked in my bed, the sheets pooling around her hips. It wasn't an image I'd soon forget, nor was it something I was going to share with this crowd.

"Kennedy," Maya said, "did Bree say how long she'd be staying? Will she be here for our Winterfest toast?"

I resisted the urge to roll my eyes at Maya's need to give everything syrupy sweet labels. What she called "Winterfest toast," the rest of us called "Meeting at the old bridge and drinking spiked hot cocoa." We did it every year at the end of Winterfest, and this year would be no different.

Or would it?

Hell, I hadn't even known Bree was coming. How would I know how long she'd be sticking around? "We haven't touched base in a while," I confessed.

"Really?" Sami frowned, looking as confused as I felt.

Last time I'd texted Bree and she'd bothered to respond, she'd said she wasn't coming home for Winterfest this year. *I'm kind of over it,* the text had said. Which had just pissed me off because I wasn't stupid. She wasn't over "it"—she was over *me*. She shouldn't punish herself and everyone who wanted to see her because of me. Because of what happened in October. She'd never missed a Winterfest.

"So, she's coming?" Christ. I sounded like a pathetic little boy asking after his celebrity crush.

Sami narrowed her eyes at me. "Aubree wouldn't miss Winterfest."

"You sure about that? She's little Miss New York City now."

Bree was also the only person I knew from Abbott Springs who understood I was more than just another Hale destined to run Hale Construction and act as Abbott Springs' mayor. I would never be as unpredictable as Bree, but she made me want to take a chance.

October be damned. I couldn't wait to see the little punk.

Aubree

Coming back to Abbott Springs was a little like putting on pajamas after a long day's work. My shoulders relaxed as the limo stopped to drop me in front of Juke's Box.

The air was crisp and the fresh snow crunched under my boots as I climbed onto the sidewalk. A block away, tiny colored lights winked at me from the town square, where they were hung for the weekend's Winterfest activities. Some long-dormant emotion tugged in my chest at the sight and I tamped it back down where it belonged. If I was going to do the whole Winterfest thing this year, I had to keep my shit together. No gushy nostalgia, no unrequited love self-pity.

I pulled open the door to the bar and was smacked in the face with the raucous sounds of Abbott Springs' only decent bar. The air was filled with the clattering of pool balls and the sounds of laughter, and the DJ set up his equipment on the backside of the dance floor.

"Aubree!" Sami called from the back. She and Maya were grinning and waving. Before I could head her way, three other people were calling me out.

"How's the big city treating you, Aubree?" someone at the pool table asked.

"Good to see your face, kid!" Juke called from behind the bar.

Craig Walton walked toward me, almost predatory, and gave me a slimy once-over. "Looking good as always, Bree. Welcome home."

I forced a smile. Home. Where was that for me? Chicago? Seattle? Manhattan? Not those. But I had my fingers crossed for Paris.

Following Craig, I pushed my way through the Friday night crowd toward my friends' table.

"Hey, Picasso. Long time no see."

The deep voice stilled my feet and punched me in the gut as I turned to look at its owner. "Kennedy."

Kennedy Hale leaned against the far side of the bar, looking even more beautiful than I remembered. He was in jeans and a long-sleeved black tee, and his shoulders seemed broader, his arms thicker. Even the scruff on his jaw was sexier than I remembered. He was an older, more sophisticated version of the boy I'd fallen hard for my sophomore year in high school. Dark, rugged, larger than life, and even sexier than in my dreams. Which was saying something. My heart pounded double-time at the sight of him, my chest aching with years of pent-up longing.

"I thought you weren't coming this year. I thought you were—what were your words?" He looked at the ceiling thoughtfully. "You were 'over it.'"

If I were only so lucky. I shrugged.

He stepped closer so we didn't have to shout to hear each other. "I thought you were too good for the rest of us."

He was angry? I guess I should have seen that coming, but it seemed…unjust. He was the one who'd rejected *me*. "I never said I was too good for anyone."

"Hmm." He took another step closer, and his scent filled my head. Damn, he smelled good. And did he get even taller? Was that possible? "You didn't have to."

"I work a lot." And I was so full of shit. I didn't work, I floundered. Job to job, relationship to relationship. Floundering was time-consuming and exhausting, and it didn't exactly make me want to meet up with my old buds and listen to them recite their successes. Everly had the band, Kennedy had football, Oliver had the bakery. I had half a dozen jobs at random tattoo parlors and a string of ex-boyfriends who were starting to make death row inmates look appealing. "It's hard for me to get home."

Kennedy raised a brow. "It's too bad your phone doesn't work."

I shook my head and signaled the bartender. "Could you make me a vodka tonic?"

"More vodka than tonic, right?" The bartender winked at me and grabbed a glass. I pulled a bill from my purse and handed it over as he slid my drink across the bar. "I'll get your change."

I waved him away. "Keep it."

Kennedy watched me as I took a drink. "Nothing changes," he muttered. "How's New York?"

I put the glass to my lips, drinking until it was over halfway gone. The bartender had done as he'd promised and made it strong. Bless him. "Amazing, of course." Amazing enough that I'd sold my loft and bought a ticket to Paris. "How's the fine Waskeegee Tech?" I asked, referring to the small private college where he played football.

"Kind of a drag."

I plastered on a smile. "I heard you have a new girlfriend."

"Funny. I heard the same about you."

This time my smile was for real.

He chuckled and snagged my drink from my hands. Our fingers brushed, and the barest contact had my stomach flip-flopping in anticipation. Obviously, my stomach was an idiot with a poor memory. My brain, on the other hand, remembered Kennedy's too-recent-for-comfort rejection all too well. But if Kennedy was going to act like that hadn't happened, so could I.

I couldn't help myself. I watched him throw back the rest of my drink, his throat working as he swallowed. Swallowing should not be sexy, but tell that to my panties.

"I'm surprised to see you here," I confessed. "I would have thought your dad would have had you running around to various Winterfest engagements."

"Ah, yes. Waving to the commoners or whatnot." He grimaced.

"I'm free until tomorrow's opening ceremony."

"If you two are going to take so long, you'd better have a beer for me when you get over here!" Craig called from the corner.

Kennedy gestured toward the table. "Your fan club awaits."

"Whatever. You're the Hale in the building. How many months before your first run for mayor?"

Something changed in his expression, but he didn't reply. Instead, he turned to the bartender and ordered beer for our table. We waited and took the pitcher and glasses ourselves before heading over.

"Bree!" Sami exclaimed as Kennedy plopped the tray on the table. "It's so good to see you!"

"You too!" She looked adorable tonight in her little pink sweater and jeans, but as I leaned in to give her a half-hug, I couldn't help but notice the stress around her eyes. Was that from college? Home? It felt weird not knowing, and the rift time and geography had put between me and my friends was all but tangible as I took my seat.

"Poker?" I asked, producing a deck of cards from my pocket. If it didn't exactly feel like old times, I'd pretend until it did.

"I'm in," Craig said.

"Why not?" said Sami.

Maya gave me a huge grin and produced a bag of poker chips. Maya was like that—always prepared to carry on the traditions you didn't even realize you had.

I looked to Kennedy, who shrugged his agreement. I tapped the cards from the pack and started shuffling as Maya divvied out the chips. I'd been playing poker with my friends for years. I loved the game, but tonight it was more than that. It gave me something to do with my hands, something to distract me while Kennedy sat so close.

"Okay, give me the scoop." I dealt, and Kennedy poured a round for everyone. "What have I missed?" I instinctively looked to Maya, who'd stayed in town and attended a local community college. They were my source for all Abbott Springs gossip.

"Bernie was arrested for indecent exposure last week," Maya

said. She made a face at her hand then added, "A group of high school boys asked her to strip for them after a basketball game, and she did. Right on the lawn in town square. In the snow."

"Are we playing for money?" Craig asked.

"No!" everyone but Kennedy said in unison. We used to play with cash but Kennedy whooped us all—every time. He was so damn careful and methodical, and it seemed to always work in his favor. He might not win every hand, but he'd inevitably win the session.

"Dad won re-election in November," Kennedy chimed in. He threw in a couple of chips for his initial bet and looked to Sami.

Sami frowned at the small pile of chips in the middle of the table and shook her head before laying her cards on the table.

Maya matched Kennedy's bet and said, "City council voted down Mrs. Winchester's proposal for mandatory Christmas decorations, but it was close."

Craig added his chips, bringing the bet to me.

I took a long pull from my beer and contemplated my cards. An unmatched seven and two. Most people would fold, but most people were boring.

"Mandatory Christmas decorations?" I tossed a few chips to the center of the table, doubling Kennedy's bet. Everyone groaned. "Mrs. Winchester proposed that?"

"Yeah, she launched this whole campaign. She called it 'Keep the Light Christmas' or something like that."

I frowned. "Isn't she Jewish?"

"She likes the tourist draw of the over-the-top decorations," Kennedy explained as he tossed in chips to call my bet. "She thinks we could capitalize on it more if everyone participated. You know, in a secular way or whatever."

Maya folded—probably before she should have—and Craig shifted in his chair and scowled at Kennedy. If I had to guess, I'd say he wanted to fold but his misplaced machismo wouldn't allow him to bow out before Kennedy. He called too, and I muttered, "So pretty much nothing's changed."

Kennedy leaned back in his chair, eyes on his cards. "It's Abbott

Springs. Nothing changes."

"How's your family, Kennedy?" Sami asked in her usual quiet voice.

"Good. Great." He shifted in his seat. His family was the face of Abbott Springs—and his father worked hard to keep it that way. I couldn't blame him for not wanting to fill the table in on the latest restoration project or community gathering his parents had funded.

I turned the river. An eight of spades, a king of hearts, and a three of clubs. Craig groaned, but Kennedy kept his typical poker face and placed a modest bet.

Craig threw his cards on the table. "I fold."

Sami folded too.

Down to just me and Kennedy. I didn't bother looking at my cards again. I knew what I had, and knowing Kennedy, I also knew there was about a one percent chance that the upcoming cards could make my hand into something that could beat him. But the chance was still there.

"All in." I pushed my chips to the center of the table.

Kennedy crossed his arms. "You're kidding me, right?"

"Nope."

He stared at me for several long beats. I smiled sweetly, hoping he couldn't hear the way my heart was slamming in my chest in response to his eyes on me.

Finally, he shook his head and threw his cards on the table. "It's all yours."

Grinning, I grabbed Kennedy's cards before he could stop me. Then the grin fell from my face. "You folded a pair of kings? Seriously?"

He shrugged. "You went all in. Logic would dictate you knew you had a winning hand. It wasn't worth the risk." He reached for my cards, but I smacked my hand on them before he could look.

"And logic made you lose," I said. I scooped all the cards together before he could pry my hand away and see I'd been betting on nothing.

Kennedy rolled his eyes.

"What did you have, Bree?" Maya asked. "I want to know."

"She won't tell," Kennedy grumbled. "Probably because it sucked."

"It doesn't matter if it sucked or not." I pulled my chips from the center of the table. "It was a winning hand."

"Who's ready for the dirty dancing contest?" the DJ asked over the big speakers, saving Kennedy from responding.

The crowd responded with its usual mix of cheers and distain, but couples were already flooding the tiny makeshift stage.

Sami looked at me expectantly, and I shook my head. "I've been traveling all day. I'm too tired."

Craig sidled closer. "Want me to help wake you up?" Craig was nice but…no.

"Watch out, Kennedy," Maya warned. "Someone's got her eye on you."

I looked up to see Bernie stumbling toward our table, her laser-like focus locked on Kennedy.

Maya and Sami exchanged a glance and snickered. Bernie liked to think herself a cougar, but the guys spent more time dodging her than anything. Her eyes were cloudy as she put her hand on Kennedy's arm. "Be my partner, sweet thing?"

He sighed and shook his head. "Man, I'm sorry, Bern. I've already promised Bree here that I'd dance with her."

I looked around the table, but no one seemed to think his forcing me to dance with him was odd. Of course, none of our friends knew what had happened in October. I, however, wasn't so lucky.

I nudged him. "That's okay. Bernie can have this one. I'll catch you next time."

Maya's eyes went wide. No doubt in shock that I was throwing Kennedy under the bus. "But you and Kennedy have won the last three years. It wouldn't be Winterfest if you two didn't dirty dance."

"Where are Kennedy Hale and Aubree Baxter?" the DJ asked, and Maya gave me a shit-eating grin that seemed to say, *"Told you so."*

Craig snorted. "Right. That's why Kennedy wants to put his

hands all over Bree. Nostalgia. I vote we mix things up. I'll dance with Bree this year."

"I don't want to—" My protest was cut short because Kennedy was already standing and pulling me from the table.

"Come on, Picasso. We can't let down the fans."

"You know the rules," the DJ said. "This is a dirty dancing competition, not obscene dancing competition. Keep it PG-thirteen, folks. Judges will circulate. If you're tapped on the shoulder, you're out. Keep dancing until you're tapped. Last couple standing wins a"—he paused a few beats and shuffled through the papers in front of him—"hell, I can't find it. Last couple standing wins a round of drinks!"

The crowd cheered, and with that, the DJ hit a switch and started the song. The walls shook with the heavy bass of a Robin Thicke hit. Kennedy's eyes were somewhere between amused and weary as he pulled me close. The alcohol in my system made it easier to press against him, easier to pretend we were just the buds we used to be *before* October.

"Mom wants you to stay at our place," he said as his hands ran down my sides and settled at the base of my spine.

I slid one hand into his back pocket and plunged the other in his hair. Our hips rocked in time to the music. "I'm perfectly fine at Dad's, but I'll make sure I visit with her before I leave."

He curled his fingers into my hips and yanked my body against his. I tilted my head to the side as he skimmed his lips along my neck. He spun me around so my back was to his front and he snaked a hand up my shirt, the rough pads of his fingers hot against the sensitive skin of my belly.

My buzz might have given me the courage to do this, but it also made it harder not to pretend that his hands on my body meant something more. I held my breath, trying to hold back the warmth pooling in my belly. There was no denying that I wanted this. I wanted to dance close to Kennedy. To have him pull me into his arms like this. But this dance was just like the rest of our relationship—one endless act of torturous foreplay for me, nothing but fun and games to him.

There was something different between us this time. The first time we'd entered the competition together, it had been a joke, but we'd moved well together. Then we'd done it again because it had been expected. This time, the tension between us as we moved to the music was entirely noticeable—and increasingly awkward.

The dance floor thinned as the judges made their way through.

He pulled back and studied me. "Are we gonna try to win this thing or not?"

Damn. Even he could tell I was phoning it in, pulling back when I should have been moving close, withdrawing from his touch when I should have been pressing into it.

The DJ blended one song into the next and transitioned into a song with a faster beat.

I flashed Kennedy a look over my shoulder and then I took his hand and pressed it against my stomach, rolling my hips to the beat. He spun me back to face him and we moved like that for a minute. The push-pull of the dance was so appropriate. I'd step away, and he'd pull me back in. He'd give me his touch and then take it away. We didn't move in tandem so much as in opposition to one another, like some long, teasing mating ritual.

The song worked its way to its crescendo and Kennedy drew my body against his. His hand wrapped around the back of my neck. His other hand found the back of my thigh, drew my leg up around his waist, and lowered me into a dip, his mouth inches from mine.

The audience clapped and cheered. I knew the applause was for us, but all I wanted was for him to mean it. The song ended and the crowd cheered as the DJ declared us the fourth-year winners. Kennedy gently released my leg and turned to shake the judges' hands.

Then he turned back to me. He gathered me into his arms and swung me around. Again, the crowd cheered. Everyone loved Kennedy. He was the town golden boy, the football star, the mayor's son. What wasn't to love?

When he settled me onto my feet again, there was a moment I thought he might kiss me. God, I wanted him to. So badly. I wanted him to delve his hands into my hair and crush his mouth against mine. I'd even settle for an innocent brushing of lips. But he didn't. He wouldn't.

I backed away, swallowing and reminding myself that indulging those fantasies did me no favors. "I had a long day," I said. "I'm gonna cut out early."

"The winners are supposed to have one more dance," he protested, tugging on my fingers to pull me back into his arms.

I was too pathetic to protest. This was Kennedy, after all. Anytime he flashed a little dimple or looked at me through those impossibly thick lashes, I was a goner.

We swayed our hips to the music and he lowered his head until his mouth hovered above my ear. His breath sent uninvited shivers of pleasure through me.

"So, are we going to pretend it didn't happen?" he asked. His voice was low and rough, and I wanted to rub against it, nuzzle it like a cat. *You've lost your mind,* some sane part of my brain told me. "Because I think we should talk about it."

My head snapped back and my eyes went wide. "Talk about what?"

"October? You showing up unannounced? Naked in my bed? Ring any bells?"

This was not the conversation I'd expected to have tonight. Didn't he want to pretend it hadn't happened even more than I did?

His dark eyes softened as he studied me, and I stiffened at his pity. I hated that he felt *sorry* for me.

"Yes," I finally said. "Yes, we're going to pretend it didn't happen. I hardly remember it anyway. You know me. I get drunk and do stupid things."

"And then you avoid my calls for months? Fuck that, Bree." I tried to escape his embrace, but he drew me tighter against him and whispered in my ear, "I'm not going to let you throw this friendship away just because you're embarrassed by some dumb drunken mistake."

Dumb drunken mistake? Five years of unrequited love and he thought the night I found the courage to act on it was a drunken mistake?

The vodka was getting to me. Or our dance was. Or both. In my half-tipsy state, I could almost imagine this conversation was going differently, going somewhere worthwhile even. Like my bed. Or fuck, against the wall in a bathroom stall here at the Juke's. I wasn't exactly picky at this point.

Was it really only three months ago that I'd flown back to Ohio to surprise Kennedy at school? I'd been so lonely. Because I didn't love my life in New York as much as I'd said I did. New York was just like Seattle, which had been just like Chicago. Same loneliness, same floundering, different skyline.

I'd been dumped by another guy from my "revolving door of men," as Kennedy liked to call them. The asshole had said I was "too unpredictable." And all I could think was that Kennedy would never say that to me, that Kennedy *liked* that about me. I'd hopped on a plane and taken a cab from the airport to his dorm. I'd sipped peppermint schnapps the whole way there, and by the time I stumbled up to his door, my nerves had melted under the heat of too much alcohol. Slipping naked into his empty bed had seemed like a good idea.

Kennedy hadn't agreed.

"Was she your girlfriend?" I asked now. "Or just a hook-up?"

His fingers toyed with my hair, and I felt his body sag as he exhaled. "Girlfriend."

"Did I ruin everything?"

He dropped his hands to his sides and studied me. We both knew I wasn't just asking about his relationship with the girl. I'd put our friendship on the line.

He shrugged. "These things have a way of working out."

My cheeks burned, but I wouldn't let myself break eye contact. "Well, for what it's worth, I'm sorry."

He nodded, but I still couldn't make out his expression.

The song found its end, and I found my excuse to escape. "I need to go home." I forced a smile. "I'm exhausted."

I waved to our friends and pushed out of the bar, Kennedy's

eyes on me the whole time. The cold air whipped at my cheeks as I walked home, sobering me. Sober and realistic was more depressing than tipsy and pathetically hopeful.

I hadn't expected him to bring up October, but I guess if I had, I'd seen it going differently. Maybe I'd imagined that if we ever talked about it, he would confess that under any other circumstances it would have been a dream come true to see me in his bed. Maybe I'd thought he'd whisper in my ear how sexy I looked naked in his bed.

How long was it going to take me to get over Kennedy Hale?

CHAPTER
Two

Kennedy

"*A*re you saving the next dance for me, handsome?"

The sound of Bernie's voice tugged me out of my reverie and made me pull my eyes off Bree's form disappearing down the street. I should have offered to walk Bree home, but after that dance I didn't trust myself to be alone with her.

Bernie wrapped her hand behind my neck, not bothering to wait for permission before inserting herself into my arms. I took her hand in mine to keep some distance between us, but I didn't have the heart to push her away again. Bernie was really harmless. She was just a lonely lady who drank too much. Not so different from Bree in some ways.

"When are you going to make things official between you and that Baxter girl?" she asked, as if reading my thoughts.

"We're just friends." It was an objection I'd been stating since we were teenagers, and it was true. I had no desire to have more than friendship with Bree.

Okay. That was a lie. There were definitely parts of me—particularly parts farther south—that wanted more than friendship with Bree. But sex was cheap. Look what it had done to my relationship with Bree's best friend Everly.

No, I'd learned my lesson. The kind of friendship I had with Bree—or *had* had before she'd pulled her little stunt in October—was priceless. It was the good bet, every time. Something I could count on. I wasn't selling it out just because the smell of her perfume could get me hard in point-oh-three seconds.

"Probably better," Bernie said, patting my cheek. "She's too much like her mama. Can't stay still. Always looking for the next adventure. Never happy to be in one place."

She was happy in Abbott Springs. She just moved because she thought she was supposed to.

My phone buzzed at my hip, and I excused myself from Bernie's arms to take the call. "Hey, Mom."

"Kennedy! Would you do me a favor and swing by Aubree's house on your way home tonight? Linus told me he had to leave on business, and I don't like her staying in that big house all alone."

Was I seriously the only one who hadn't known Aubree was coming into town? "Sure, but I saw her at Juke's a few minutes ago. She said she was fine staying at her dad's."

"She was just being polite," Mom scolded. "Go get her and bring her here where she belongs."

"I'll see what I can do," I promised. My mom loved Bree like one of her own—perhaps more than her own. After Bree's mom had skipped town, Bree spent many of her nights at our house. Her relationship with my parents made me jealous as hell. While my parents insisted I live life on their terms, their surrogate daughter got away with everything. Tattoos, drinking, older men. Mom had always just winked and let it slide. Maybe she'd never objected because she didn't have any claim to Bree. Or maybe it was just because Bree was Bree, and stifling her boldness would be like blotting out a shining star.

"Thanks, sweetie. And don't forget, we have lunch with the board on Saturday. I know you want to spend time with your friends this weekend, but your dad is counting on you being there."

I groaned. The last thing I wanted was to go to some fancy

dinner and have the men talk about my future like it was their own. Maybe if Bree came, she could keep the subject more neutral. Maybe if Bree came, I wouldn't hate every minute of it. Further evidence that the best thing we could be for each other was friends.

"Oh, and I hope you don't mind, but I put the air mattress in your room. Your sisters have friends over for the weekend, and they've taken up residence in the guest bedroom."

"You're going to make Bree sleep on an air mattress?" I really wanted to ask if she was *out of her freaking mind.* What kind of mother put a girl like Bree in her son's bedroom? Did she want me to screw up everything? I squeezed my eyes shut, trying to block out all of the all-too-vivid scenarios playing out in my head. Oh, the possibilities.

"No, Kennedy," Mom corrected, "you take the air mattress. She can sleep in your bed."

"Mom, I'm not sure that's appropriate."

"Nonsense. We all know you wouldn't do anything inappropriate."

Aubree

The walk from Juke's to my childhood home was short, but the wind was wicked. By the time I entered the house through the garage, punching in the code to disable the alarm, the cold had sunk deep into my bones.

"Hello?" I called. I already knew my dad wasn't here, but I wasn't sure if the maid would be around.

When my plane landed in Cleveland, I'd turned on my phone to find a text from him: *Sorry, kid. I had to take care of some last-minute business in Hong Kong. I hired a limo to meet you and bring you to Abbott Springs.*

A limo. I hadn't seen my father in a year—he'd barely made it home at last Winterfest before I had to leave again—and all I got when I came home was a fucking limo. That was my relationship with him. He gave me everything money could buy, and all I really wanted was a hug. So, you know, your basic clichéd poor little rich girl.

I made my way through the servants' kitchen to the back staircase and up to my old room. I knew what I'd find there. Furniture gleaming from a fresh polish, the bed, newly made with a fluffy down comforter, maybe even some fresh flowers on the dresser. And all the loneliness an only child could ask for.

I hit the landing and my footsteps echoed through the empty space.

God, I hated this house. I knew my father did too. There were too many reminders here. Everything was exactly as Mom had left it. I wished he would sell it, but part of him still believed she might come back.

"Must run in the family," I muttered, pushing through my bedroom door.

I was exhausted from traveling all day and second-thinking my decision to come at all. The unexpected time with Kennedy had left me feeling blindsided. The memory of his hands on me during our dance had left me feeling something else altogether. I just wanted to warm up and wash the travel-yuck off myself before getting a solid night's sleep.

The bathroom attached to my bedroom was stocked with Aveda products for my arrival. Dad probably thought I used this stuff year round in New York, but I couldn't afford it. He would have written a check if he'd known that, but I'd spent the last six months living under the delusion that I could make it on my own. It was bad enough that he'd financed every move without qualm, never making a peep about me settling down. Would that change when I told him about Paris? Maybe. Or maybe he'd be happy that I got her back in my life.

I turned the water as hot as I could stand it and stripped while it warmed. When I stepped under the spray and closed my eyes, I let the water pressure hammer at my loneliness. I should've been used to coming home to an empty house. I should've been used to the push-pull tug of hope and disappointment being home inspired.

We'd had a dog when I was a kid. His name was Paws because I'd gotten him when I was eight and apparently had no imagination when it came to naming pets.

Paws would jump the fence and go down to Abbott's Sweet Confections and raid their dumpster for day-old chocolate cookies and muffins and Danishes. He would get miserably sick every time, and he'd lie on the patio afterward and look up at me with those big brown eyes, just begging me to make it better. But despite his misery and our attempts to prevent his escapes, he did it again and again. As if he couldn't resist the siren call of day-old chocolate baked goods.

This trip home reminded me of Paws's dumpster raids. An irresistible, joyful treat that would only end in misery and self-loathing.

I had gone so far as to tell Kennedy I wasn't coming home for the festival this year, but much like Paws, I was weak. When Everly called and told me she was going to perform here, I'd known it was the perfect excuse. I'd wanted to see my friends and remember the good old days. I'd wanted to see Kennedy and *forget* October.

Unfortunately, he wasn't going to let me.

I scrubbed my scalp and exfoliated my limbs to within an inch of my life, and by the time I turned off the water, my skin was humming.

I grabbed a towel off the heated rack and ran the plush terry cloth over my skin before tucking it under my arms and heading through the bathroom door to the bedroom.

"Did you decide to save some water for the rest of the town after all?"

I jumped at the sound of Kennedy's voice and clutched at the towel wrapped under my arms. "Holy shit! You scared the daylights out of me!"

He kept his eyes on my face. Of course he did. But I was standing there in a freaking towel, and I would have thought he'd at least *look* at my legs or the way the towel clung to my breasts or…something. There I stood, weak in the knees just because he didn't shave this morning, and he didn't have the courtesy to sneak a peek?

I was pathetic.

So. Pathetic.

"Get dressed. Mom is pacing the floors. She won't sleep until she knows you're safe in under her roof."

"Seriously?" Once, shortly after Mom had left, our house had been robbed while Dad was out of town and I was in my room. I'd heard them downstairs, scrounging through our stuff, and I'd called the police with shaking hands. After that, I'd started staying at the Hales' while Dad was away.

"Seriously," he said, crossing his arms and not once dropping his gaze to my better assets.

Paws, I thought, *I totally get you.*

CHAPTER
Three

Kennedy

ree was gorgeous. A goddess. This wasn't news to me. Despite what she thought, I'd noticed. Fuck, had I noticed. I'd noticed before seeing her in that little towel, and I'd noticed before she'd climbed into my bed in October.

After her mom skipped town, she'd slept more of her high school nights in the room next to mine than she had in her own home. What guy in his right mind wouldn't notice Bree? What teenage boy wouldn't lie in his bed and imagine her sleeping in hers? What hot-blooded male wouldn't notice the want to slide into bed with her and explore her tight curves?

Yeah. I'd noticed. I'd noticed the way she arched her back when she yawned and that she didn't sleep with a bra. When she'd stay at my parents' house, I'd see her light on at night and make up an excuse to come to her. She had no idea how hard I had to fight not to stare at the way her nipples pebbled under her T-shirt. And the nights one of her nightmares would wake her and she'd climb into my bed?

Fuck, yes. I'd noticed everything, down to the look in her

eyes when I'd told her to get dressed. Was it hurt? Vulnerability? Whatever it was, it had hit me hard, like a red-hot fist to the solar plexus.

God, she was gorgeous. Icy blue eyes framed by thick, dark lashes. The hard angles of her jaw only accentuated the plump pink softness of her lips. Even the glint of the little stone in her nose piercing was sexy. She was always changing her hair, but this week it was dark with thick platinum streaks in the curls that hit her shoulders—plus, of course, her signature red streak through the bit that was perpetually falling into her eyes.

Wanting her was nothing new. But somehow, until she'd shown up unannounced at my dorm, I'd always missed the way she looked at me.

Eventually, Bree was going to quit moving around the country like a lost soul and move back to Abbott Springs. When that happened, we'd both be glad we hadn't ruined our friendship by acting on this attraction between us.

"You know how Mom feels about you staying here alone," I explained awkwardly, struggling to act like her semi-nude state was no big deal as she scrounged through her bag for clothes.

"Okay, okay," she muttered. She strode back into the bathroom, and I squeezed my eyes shut, half-hard and wishing I hadn't noticed the few drops of water slowly trailing their way down her thighs.

By the time she emerged, I was already scooping her bag off the floor and throwing the strap over my shoulder.

"Kennedy," she objected. She tried to grab the bag off my shoulder, but I held fast. "Fine, Macho Man. Carry the damn bag."

I couldn't help but smile. Girls were always trying to be so proper and sweet around me. Not Bree. Never Bree. I missed that. Didn't she get that I *needed* that? I needed people in my life who would give it to me straight. I needed Bree, who lived life on her own terms. I needed her to stand by me while I took a stab at doing the same.

My smile fell away as she walked down the hall and my eyes glued themselves to the sexy swish of her ass in those tiny black pants she slept in.

I gritted my teeth and averted my eyes. I wasn't going to add another nail to the coffin of our friendship by letting her catch me ogling her ass. I was pretty sure feeling her up during that stupid dance contest had pushed my limits enough. And having her sleep in my bedroom tonight? I was contemplating a night on the couch.

As I followed her downstairs, I didn't look at her ass once. Four or five times? Maybe.

"I need a snack before we go." She hit a switch on the wall and flooded the kitchen with light. "Dad said he had the maid stock the fridge."

I pulled open the fridge and studied the contents. Chocolate milk, Lunchables, chocolate pudding. "You eat like a four-year-old." I moved to the pantry and found a basket labeled "Bree" with Cocoa Puffs, Pop-Tarts, and Doritos. After grabbing the chips, I joined her at the island, where she was already opening up a bottle of chocolate milk and a container of pudding. "I can't believe you still eat this crap. Most girls would kill to be able to eat junk food all the time and have your body."

She waved away the compliment and dug into the Doritos. "Mom used to be like this, but she said it caught up with her about the time she hit twenty-five. I figure I've gotta enjoy it while I can."

"How is your mom anyway?" I asked. "Is she still living in LA?"

She shook her head faintly, her teeth sinking into her bottom lip. "She's moving to Paris."

Shit. Leave it to Bree's mom to put an ocean between herself and her daughter.

"I'm sorry," I muttered. "That sucks."

She nodded but kept her eyes locked on her glass of chocolate milk.

"Do you want to talk about it?"

Her smile was strained when she said, "What's there to talk about?"

Aubree

This was probably an opportune time to tell Kennedy about my move. Mama didn't raise a coward, so I lifted my eyes to meet his and took a breath. Only the words that came out of my mouth had nothing to do with my plans. "How's your dad?"

It was Kennedy's turn to avoid eye contact now. We didn't used to be like this. We told each other everything. Had I ruined that? He kept his eyes trained on some invisible point behind my head. "He's already set up my desk at the office. He's ready for me to graduate, move home, work at the business, and eventually step into his shoes as mayor."

That sounded miserable. Kennedy deserved more than to live a carbon copy of someone else's life. But I just said, "Wow. That's amazing."

"Right. I'm the luckiest guy in town, I guess."

I dropped my Doritos halfway to my mouth. The man had such a good poker face that I could never read him. This was no exception, but I didn't need to be able to read him to know he didn't want his father's life. "Could we drop the bullshit?"

He frowned. "Why are you the only one who knows I'm more than the next piece of the 'Hale legacy'?" He made air quotes around the last words.

I didn't have an answer for that.

He stared at me for several long beats before he spoke. "My coach at Waskeegee thinks I have a chance at the pros." He broke his chip into five tiny pieces. "I probably wouldn't be drafted, coming from a no-name football school, but he thinks I could get on a team's practice squad and work to get noticed."

Something funny was happening with my stomach—this twisting, curling, flip-flopping of nerves and excitement. Never, not once had I pushed Kennedy into taking his football talent more seriously. When he'd chosen to go to Waskeegee because of their excellent business and political science programs, I'd kept my mouth shut instead of pointing out the equally amazing opportunities at Big Ten schools, where he might make a name for himself. When he played along with his dad's plans to make Kennedy the next Abbott Springs mayor, I'd bitten my tongue instead of asking what he'd do with his love of football. Kennedy had enough people making all his life decisions for him. He didn't need to add me to the mix. But if he *wanted* to try to go pro, if it was *his* idea, that was something else altogether.

He swallowed so hard I could hear it. "You think I'm crazy, don't you."

"I think you're finally making plans that make sense for *you* instead of everyone else." I reached across the bar and put my hand over his. Our fingers intertwined, and my already spastic stomach nearly lost its shit. "You have to follow your passions, Kennedy. Abbott Springs and the family business will always be here, but the chance to play pro ball? Unlike a lot of dreams, there's a timestamp on that. You have to try now."

"I might not make it. They might not want me, even on a practice squad."

I shrugged. "I'd rather know I tried than wonder."

"It's just that simple with you, isn't it?"

"Why shouldn't it be? It's your life."

He grunted. "Tell that to my dad."

"I will," I promised. "If this is really what you want, I'll be there when you tell him, and I will happily remind him that this is *your* life, not his." I couldn't handle the closeness anymore, so I extricated my hand from his and stood to put my dishes in the sink. "Ready?"

"If you are."

Kennedy led the way out the back door and two houses over to his parents', my second home growing up.

"Bree!" Mrs. Hale threw her arms around me the second we pushed through the side entrance to her home. She drew me into her in a hard hug. "It's so good to see you, sweetheart!"

I will not cry. I will not cry. "It's good to see you too," I whispered, and in my voice I could hear the tears I refused to let in my eyes. There are two kinds of family: the people who share your blood, and the people who share your life. For years, the Hales fell into the second category for me, and I had no good excuse for neglecting them.

"I hope you don't mind me sending Kennedy to get you. I just couldn't stand the idea of you sleeping there. Thanks for humoring an old lady."

"I wanted to see you anyway," I said, shaking my head. In all honestly, I was relieved she'd insisted I come over here. I hated being alone in that big house.

"I didn't even have to physically restrain her to make her come home with me," Kennedy said dryly.

"Of course I'm selfishly thrilled that I get you for the weekend, though I am sorry you won't see your father." She took my hand in one of hers and grabbed my bag with the other.

I followed her up the stairs, my heart aching at the familiar scent of the only place that ever felt like home. The hardwood floors were polished to a shine and the air smelled of fresh flowers.

"I'm sure Kennedy explained why you'll need to share his room tonight."

CHAPTER
Four

Aubree

I nearly tripped over the last step and had to grab the handrail to right myself. "Um. Actually—"

"I'll just sleep in the den, Mom," Kennedy said behind me.

"That's not necessary," I said, thinking I should be the one to sleep on the couch.

Mrs. Hale misunderstood and nodded. "See, it's no big deal, Kennedy." Then she led the way to Kennedy's bedroom. We followed, bringing along the elephant of awkwardness between us. "I'll let you get settled," she continued, putting my bag on the bed. There was something sad in her eyes.

"Listen, I know you were hoping I'd make it for Christmas. I just—" I shook my head. How many times had I gone over this conversation in my head on the plane ride over? How many platitudes had I tested, only to decide there was nothing to say? I'd been hiding from holidays in Abbott Springs since I left. Holidays made me want to come home for good, and coming home made me feel like a failure.

"Don't you worry about it." She took my face in both of her hands, and her eyes filled. "I hear your mom's going to make it home for the festival this year."

My chest filled. "Finally." I couldn't help but smile. Mom had promised to come back every year since the year she'd left when I was fifteen, and she'd always changed plans at the last minute, too busy in her life of glitz and glamour. Whether she was leading or chasing that life, I wasn't sure.

Intellectually, I understood my mom was as likely to bail on Winterfest this year as she had every other year, but there was still a little girl inside me who thought maybe this was the year she'd show. It didn't matter though. When I moved to Paris, I'd see her all the time.

"What can I get you?" Mrs. H asked. "A bedtime snack?"

"I'm craving hot chocolate," I confessed. "I can't find a cup of hot chocolate anywhere in New York as good as yours."

"Of course you can't," she said with a smile. "I'll meet you downstairs."

She shuffled out of the room, leaving Kennedy and me alone with our pet elephant, Mr. Awkward Pants.

We spoke at the same time. "I don't have to—"

He put up a hand. "You're the guest. Take the bed."

I looked pointedly to the made-up air mattress in the corner of the room and shook my head. It didn't matter. He'd made it more than clear that he didn't see me that way. "You can stay in here. You know your sisters will wake you up before dawn if you sleep downstairs."

His blue eyes grew serious, and for the four hundred and ninety-eighth time since arriving back in town a few hours ago, I wished I knew what he was thinking.

"I'm going to go down for some hot chocolate." Though I knew I wouldn't be able to stomach it right now. The craving making a mess of my insides was for sex, not sweets.

Mrs. Hale met me at the foot of the stairs. She'd probably been waiting there this whole time. She squeezed my arm and pulled me closer, threading her arm through mine as we walked into the kitchen. "Can I tell you something?"

I wasn't very good with emotions and stuff, and I knew that was what was coming. Mrs. Hale was all about the emotions. "Um. Okay."

"I'm worried about Kennedy. I don't think he's happy. He's distant, and as anxious as we are to have him back home, I don't think he's ready to leave school."

I reminded my feet to keep moving forward and trained my face into a mask of respectably detached concern. The truth was, I wanted to spill the beans to his mom. She'd understand why Kennedy needed to go after his dream, and she'd stand behind him even if—when—her husband threatened to disown his son.

"Do you think you can talk to him?" she asked. "Feel him out? See if there's anything we can do or something we should know?"

I settled into a kitchen chair and watched her as she poured thick cream into a pan and placed it on the stove.

"I don't think he'll want to talk to me," I objected.

She gathered sugar and cocoa from the cupboards. "Kennedy doesn't talk to anyone, and you know how intense his dad can be. He's all expectations, all the time. But I know if Kennedy is going to open up, it will be to you." She shook her head and forced a smile. "Enough about that. Let's talk about you. Are you still seeing that young man I met when I was in the city?"

"Ramey?" Had I seriously introduced my emo, nihilist ex to a woman sweeter than hot cocoa? "No, he's not in the picture anymore."

"Do you still love the city? Think you'll stay?"

I swallowed. "Actually, I'm not going back to New York. After Winterfest, I'm moving to Paris with my mom."

"Paris?" The word was a choked question from the other side of the kitchen.

We both turned to see Kennedy, his hands tucked into his flannel sleep pants.

"To live?" he asked.

"For college," I said. "Mom wants me to live with her while I get my degree." I wished he'd look angry or disappointed. Anything but that blank expression that revealed nothing.

He shouldn't have found out this way.

"You must be so excited," Mrs. Hale enthused. "Paris, the city of love. And you'll get more time with your mom too. That'll be nice."

Kennedy

*P*aris. She was going to *Paris*. Was I supposed to be happy she was going to live with her mom and not just relocating to follow another guy in her string of losers? Instead, knowing she was going to live with her mom made it worse. Because it made it more permanent somehow.

"Congratulations," I said, but the word sounded strained even to my own ears. We both knew I was full of shit. "That's great."

"I'm excited. I've applied to these art schools and if I get in, it would be an amazing experience."

If she got in? I bit back my criticism. That was just like Bree to relocate to a different country for college when she didn't even know if she'd been accepted to said college yet. And the fact that this entire decision relied on her mom?

"Do you want some cocoa, Kennedy?" Mom asked as she handed a steaming mug to me.

"No. I just came down to say goodnight."

"Goodnight, dear," Mom said.

"I'll try to be quiet when I come in," Bree whispered. Her eyes were sad, and I knew she was disappointed in my reaction to her news. She was moving to Paris. How had she expected me to respond?

I excused myself and headed upstairs, where I climbed under the covers on the air mattress and stared at the ceiling in the darkness.

If I'd handled things differently in October, would Paris still be in Bree's plans? I'd handled it horribly when I realized who the naked girl in my bed was, and I'd handled it horribly tonight.

Bringing it up at Juke's had been careless. I should have thought it through before I broached the subject. I just didn't understand what she wanted from me. She was all about taking the risk and going with the flow. She leaped before she looked. Case in point? Paris.

It wasn't long before I heard the soft creaking of the stairs and Aubree coming into the room. She didn't turn on any lights, but I could make out her silhouette as she grabbed her bag and headed into the bathroom.

When she came back and climbed into my bed, I thought about climbing in after her. What would it be like to be carefree like her? To take a chance when every indicator said you would fail?

"Kennedy? Are you awake?" she whispered.

I squeezed my eyes shut and didn't answer. I wanted her too much, and the news of her move had left me too raw.

Aubree

Either he was sleeping or he wasn't speaking to me. Fine. What could I say anyway? *Hey, if you would've fucked me silly instead of freaking out back in October, maybe I'd stick around?*

Not only was that ridiculous, it wasn't true. If Kennedy had responded like I'd wanted him to, if he would've given us a chance, it'd probably all be over by now. Because that was what happened with me. I screwed things up.

The LED light flashed on my phone from the bedside table, letting me know I had a text.

I grabbed it and grinned when I saw it was from Everly. *Jubby just told me the funniest thing about Bernie. Did you know she got caught stripping on the courthouse lawn?*

Poor Bernie—nothing stayed quiet in Abbott Springs. I tapped out my reply. *Heard tonight. I'm back in town. Staying at Kennedy's, as per usual since Dad is MIA (also as per usual).*

Kennedy's? Well, don't let him sleep with you. He'll act like it never happened.

My teeth clenched as I read her reply. No matter how many years and miles between myself and that moment I'd seen him making love to her by the lake, I never managed to escape that horrible feeling in my gut every time I thought about them together.

Kennedy just made it worse with all his talk of her. How he screwed up. How he wished he hadn't cared so much about his parents' approval. How he never meant to hurt her.

Everly had slept with Kennedy at Winterfest last year. Sex, by the lake, in January. Yes, alcohol had been involved. When he proceeded to act like nothing had changed between them, she didn't take it well. To say she carried a grudge would be like saying Winterfest was a *little* cheesy. Winterfest was complete cheese balls, and Everly thought Kennedy was the anti-Christ for what he did to her. I totally got that Kennedy had hurt her, and I had gone through my own phase where I was angry about it—not that I'd admitted that to either of them. But the more I thought about it—and trust me, I thought about my unrequited crush having sex with my best friend far more than I'd ever admit—the more I realized that his reaction was typical Kennedy.

A pink-haired Abbott, Everly didn't fit into Kennedy's dad's plan for his son, and as such, Kennedy had saved Everly from a world of hurt by skirting a relationship with her. I was jealous of that. Because Kennedy's parents would probably love nothing more than for him to end up with me. I might have been a little wilder than their son, but I was a Baxter, and old money mattered more than tattoos and the color of your hair in this town. The idea that he *could* be with me just made the fact that he wouldn't hurt that much more.

I waited a few minutes before composing my reply, but I settled for something simple. *It's been a whole year, Ev. Either tell him how much he hurt you or let it go.*

She didn't reply, and I lay in the dark, thinking of October and wondering if I needed to take my own advice.

Tell him how much he hurt you or let it go.

Everyone thought I was brave for moving wherever my whims took me, for chasing whatever I fancied at the moment, but they didn't understand that was all cowardice in disguise. Maybe I was brave enough to show up at Kennedy's dorm, but I was too chicken to admit to him why I'd been there, to tell him how much his dismissal had hurt. I couldn't. It would be like opening myself up and handing him salt to pour into the wound.

October. I didn't want to think about October. I squeezed my eyes shut and prayed for sleep to anesthetize me to my own heartache.

CHAPTER
Five

Aubree–October

I only stumbled a little as I climbed the stairs to Kennedy's dorm. Maybe I was loopy from lack of sleep, or maybe it was the peppermint schnapps getting to me, but I couldn't wipe the grin from my face. I was finally going to do this. I was finally going to tell Kennedy how I felt about him.

I knocked on the door to his quad and propped myself up on the frame while I waited for someone to answer. It could have been a minute or an hour later that a scruffy-faced blond opened the door.

"Can I help you?" he asked.

"Oh, hey there." I recognized Kennedy's broad-shouldered roommate from pictures on Facebook. Tim? Tom? Some all-American three-letter name like that. He was part of Kennedy's offensive line, but he looked like he had no idea who I was. "I'm Bree?" I giggled when it came out as a question. As if I was so drunk I wasn't even sure of my own name.

"Oh, Bree. From Abbott Springs?"

"The one and only," I sing-songed. I attempted a little curtsy but nearly fell over.

Tim/Tom steadied me with a big hand on my arm. "Easy there."

Pushing to my tiptoes, I peeked over his head into the common space of the quad. "Is Kennedy around?"

He shook his head. "Sorry. I'm not sure where he is." He pulled the door wide and gestured me inside. "You want me to give him a call?"

I waved away the suggestion as I sauntered into the tiny apartment. "I want to *surprise* him." I giggled again. Damn. I wasn't the giggling type. "I'll just wait for him in his room," I said, heading toward the first of the four doors branching off the living area.

"Um, that's my room," Tim/Tom said.

"Oopsie!" Another giggle slipped from my lips. Okay, so I'd probably overdone it on that peppermint schnapps I'd been sipping since I got off the plane.

"Not that you're not welcome there. You absolutely are." He winked at me. He was cute. Really cute. Not like Kennedy. No, Kennedy wasn't even cute. He was panty-dropping *sexy*.

Kennedy. I grinned stupidly just thinking about what was about to happen. Finally.

"Which one is Kennedy's?" I asked.

"Back right."

"Awesome. Thanks."

"Can I get you anything?" he asked as I headed for Kennedy's door. Who knew walking in a straight line could be so much fun? Like the balance beam as a kid. *Whee.* "Maybe water or something to eat?"

So I could sober up and lose my nerve? Hardly. "I'm good, Tim/Tom," I slurred. "Don't need a thing."

I pushed into Kennedy's room and shut the door behind me. It smelled like him in here. That shouldn't have taken me by surprise. His smell was just an amalgamation of his shampoo, aftershave, and laundry detergent, so it made sense that it would follow him to school. And yet it reminded me so much of his bedroom at home that it almost stole my courage.

I walked around the small space, running my fingers over the shirts hanging in his closet, peeking at the stack of textbooks on his desk and the graded term paper in the trash. An A-. He probably hated that minus. Such a smarty pants.

Kennedy was the guy who had rallied our tiny high school's football team for the last quarter victory. He was the guy who'd received straight A's while working part time for his father's company and volunteering on weekends. He was preppy and reliable and he didn't make mistakes. But me? Mistakes were my bag, and the only A I'd known in school was the A in "See me *after* class."

Would he see my being here tonight as just another impulsive screw-up in a long line of Bree Baxter screw-ups? Or could he put his practical self aside for one night and give in to the sexual tension that had been simmering between us since we were teenagers?

The initial buzz of being in his space was wearing off, and I sank to the edge of his bed. I'd lost my job in New York City, and in true Kennedy problem-solving fashion, he'd spent half of last weekend on the phone with me trying to convince me to come back to Ohio for college.

"You could make it home to Abbott Springs more often," he'd said. "It'll be like old times. I miss your face, Bree."

No. After five years of "just friends," it was time. I wanted more from Kennedy. A lot more.

"All or nothing," I murmured. Then I took off my clothes. Everything—my shirt, my jeans, my bra, and my panties. I threw them all into a rumpled pile in the corner and slid into his bed.

I imagined his reaction at finding me here. His shock. His disbelief. And finally his arousal. I imagined him pulling back the sheets and his eyes touring my nude form. I imagined the look on his face as he fought the need to touch me and then me extending my hand and inviting him to lose that fight once and for all.

In my mind, Kennedy was mine. He just didn't know it yet.

I wished he would hurry and come home so we could get to the good part already. My peppermint schnapps buzz was taking me through that inevitable shift from tipsy to sleepy, and the scent of his aftershave on his pillow made me so relaxed that my eyes started to float closed.

I drifted in and out of sleep, my dreams a patchwork quilt of memories and fantasies.

Memory. Kennedy's arms around me after a nightmare, my back pressed into his solid chest as he whispered soothing words into my ear and I floated back to sleep. *"I've got you. It's going to be okay."*

Fantasy. His fingers dipping past the waistband of my sleep pants. His reassuring whispers turning to hesitant requests. *"Let me touch you, Bree. I've wanted this for so long."*

Memory. Kennedy's hands on my ass as we competed in the unofficial Abbott Springs dirty dancing competition. His lips parted, his mouth grazing my neck, and his body moving in time with mine.

Fantasy. Him finding me in the bathroom after and pushing me against the wall until I felt the hard length of his erection pressing into my stomach. *"Can we stop pretending?"*

Memory wove into fantasy until sleep overtook me completely, and my dreams wove my fantasies into a vivid tapestry of comfort and eroticism. I dreamed I woke up with Kennedy's arms around me and it was morning. Before I could move, his hand was between my legs and his mouth was on my neck, his whisper in my ear. *"I'm going to die if I can't be inside you soon, Bree."*

A flood of light jerked me from sleep. I wanted to draw up the covers and go back to the dream. I wanted to send away the noisy light-bearers, whoever they were, but then I heard Kennedy's voice and sat up in bed before I even remembered where I was.

"Who are you?" I asked, my eyes heavy, my voice crackling with sleep. Was I in Kennedy's house or—

It all came back to me. My impulsive flight to Ohio. The cab ride to Kennedy's small college. His roommate showing me to his room.

But this wasn't my plan, falling asleep, being disoriented. I'd never planned for the leggy blonde standing next to Kennedy, her eyes bugging out so much I feared they might pop out of her head.

I blinked at her. Trying to understand why she might be here. Then two things happened at once: I remembered I was naked, and the blonde turned to Kennedy and slapped him across the face.

"What the *fuck*, Bree?" Kennedy growled. The blonde was already storming out of his room, and from the anger on his face, I could only assume her exit didn't exactly work with his plans for the evening.

His words hurt, but not as much as the aggravation on his face. I guess I'd thought he'd find me nude in his bed and say something like, "Finally," before pressing his mouth to mine and pulling his clothes off as quickly as possible.

Instead, he said, "Jesus, are you drunk? Put some clothes on." Then he stomped out of the room. Running after his girlfriend, I could only guess.

I scrambled out of bed and dressed with shaking hands, dying inside with bone-deep embarrassment. I wasn't the kind of girl who threw herself at guys who weren't interested. I gave myself to losers and bad boys who might never hold down a steady job, but at least they wanted me. Not Kennedy. *Put some clothes on.* So much for smooth seduction.

Tim/Tom was on the couch when I cracked Kennedy's door and peeked into the common area. "Is he out there?"

"He ran after Kelsey. What happened?"

I shook my head, not trusting myself to speak. "Thanks," I managed before I ran through the common room and out the door.

I took a cab back to the Cincinnati airport, where I waited on standby for a flight back to New York. Five times my phone buzzed and Kennedy's face came up on the display. Five times I sent his call to voicemail.

I was too crushed to hear his voice, too embarrassed to explain.

Kennedy

Mom woke me up with a knock on my door just like I was in high school again, and I rolled over and buried my face in my pillow until she went away. I hadn't slept for shit last night. When Bree had tiptoed out of the room as soon as the sun peeked in through the curtains, I hadn't followed her.

I could hear her downstairs, no doubt chatting with the fam over a cup of coffee and laughing with my little sisters over some stupid joke. I climbed out of bed and went straight to the bathroom, showering and dressing before I could muster the energy to pretend everything was okay.

Today was the opening ceremony for Winterfest, and my dad would expect all of us kids to stand by his side as he gave his officious little speech. I swear, you'd think he was fucking President of the United States the way he treated his job as mayor of Abbott Springs.

After pulling on jeans and a sweater, I headed down the stairs.

Aubree was in her pajamas. She'd pulled a hooded sweatshirt over her tee, but I had an excellent view of her ass in those tight little black pants she liked to sleep in. She had the sexiest bedhead of any girl I'd ever met. No matter how she was wearing her hair, she always climbed out of bed looking half wild and freshly fucked. *I* wanted to make her hair look like that. And I'd spent the better part of my night resisting the urge.

She was laughing about something and her smile faltered as she looked up from her coffee and spotted me. "Good morning, Kennedy," she said softly.

"Kennedy!" Mom called. "Are you helping Cynthia set up for this afternoon's treasure hunt?"

I strode past both women and poured myself a cup of coffee. "Yeah. I'm meeting her at Village Hall in an hour."

"Do you need any help?" Mom asked. "Bree was just saying she doesn't have anything planned for the day. I'm sure you two want to spend as much time together as possible before she leaves the country."

Bree's cheeks flushed such a pretty pink I wanted to touch them.

"Sure," I said. "I'm sure Cynthia would really appreciate it."

"And don't forget lunch with the board tomorrow." She looked at her watch and shook her head. "I'm supposed to be helping set up the craft fair in fifteen minutes, so I need to get out of here."

Then she scurried out of the kitchen, leaving Aubree and me alone with the awkward silence.

"I'm sorry I didn't tell you about Paris," she said softly. "You shouldn't have had to find out like that."

My jaw ached from gritting my teeth and I tried to relax it. "Why are you moving?"

She shrugged. "Why not?"

I'm sure there were at least half a dozen good reasons, but the only one that would find its way to my tongue was *me*. "What cards were you holding last night?"

"What?"

"When you went all in. What cards did you have in your hand?"

She lifted her chin. "A seven and a two."

The confession shouldn't have surprised me, but it was still like a punch to the gut. "Suited?"

"No. Two of diamonds, seven of clubs."

"There you go," I muttered. "Paris in a nutshell."

She gaped, the tiny little stone in her nose winking at me. "Are you trying to compare my life to a stupid game of poker? That's real fucking nice."

"I wouldn't have to if you didn't play at both like you were trying to lose."

Her eyes flashed and she set her mug down on the counter with a clatter. "What's that supposed to mean?"

"Come on. When was the last time you could trust your mom to follow through on anything she promised you?" I was too angry to regret the words, even as hurt slashed across her delicate features. I wanted her to be hurt, damn it. I wanted her to wake up and think about what she was doing before she made a terrible mistake.

"I flew out to see her in LA in November. She took me to the set of her boyfriend's movie—just like she promised."

"Yeah, but that was about *her*. And when you moved to Seattle with the guy who wanted to live in that hippie commune? And then Chicago and then New York? It was always about *them*. You bend over backwards for people who only care about themselves and you're leaving behind people who care about you."

"Like who? Who's here that I need to stick around for? Everyone has their own life, their own plans."

"And what about me?" My voice cracked like a pre-pubescent boy when the words came out. "I'll be here."

She swallowed, some emotion I couldn't identify filling her eyes as she stared at me. "Yeah, you'll be here and be completely miserable while you live your life for someone else."

I stepped back. She was right but she didn't understand. How could she? "At least I'll succeed at something."

"Is it really success if you don't even want it?"

"Stop turning this around on me," I growled. Damn it, why couldn't she see sense? And why did I want so badly to kiss away the hurt on her face? "We're talking about you making another stupid, impulsive decision. I don't want to see you hurt."

"You don't get to turn me down flat and then guilt trip me for not sticking around." She kept her voice quiet but her words were heavy with hurt.

"Turn you down?" I fought to keep from yelling. My family didn't need to be part of this conversation. "You were drunk. I didn't—"

"Kennedy!" Mom called from the front of the house. "Cynthia is here! She needs you to ride with her downtown so you can help her set up the snow fort station."

I grabbed my thermos of coffee and headed for the door. "I have to go, but this conversation isn't over."

CHAPTER
Six

Kennedy

"Come on, son," my father called. "It's time for the opening ceremony."

The clock on Village Hall read 11:57. I squeezed my eyes shut in frustration. I had no desire to climb onto that stage with Mom and Dad and my little sisters, no desire to be the good son who nodded at my father's droning on as if he were the wise lord of the land he liked to pretend to be.

Mom stepped up and squeezed my bicep. "We'll just imagine the everyone in the crowd in their underwear," she whispered with a wink.

I grinned. Mom played along with Dad's pomp and self-importance, but she never took herself or our family too seriously. She was probably the only reason I hadn't grown up to be a self-involved asshat.

We climbed the steps of Village Hall, first Dad with Grandma at his side, then my sisters, giggling and checking their hair, then Mom and me behind. Dad took his place behind the podium and adjusted the microphone. I pasted on a smile and looked out across the sea of winter hats as he began his usual speech. I'd listened to this all my life and if I had to step in, I could recite his usual speech verbatim. *Thank you all for coming, proud moment, blah, blah, I'm the most awesomesauce mayor ever in the history of mayors.* Maybe not that last part, but it was close.

"We even have a special treat," my father added when the applause had died down a bit. "A couple of our very own hometown kids and their band, External Resurrection, will be playing tomorrow night!"

My heart skittered to a halt. No doubt, he was referring to Internal Insurrection, Everly's band. And no doubt *that* was what had brought Bree to town. She wasn't here for us. She was here for her BFF and partner in punk crime. She rarely missed Everly's shows.

I wanted to be annoyed that no one had told me about Everly's band playing, but I hadn't concerned myself with Winterfest planning much this year, and it was my own fault I didn't know.

That same old awkward feeling I got every time I thought about Everly washed over me. Damn. I'd really screwed that up. She was just so sweet and…breakable behind her punk rocker façade. I was like the kid who knew he shouldn't have played with mom's precious china but couldn't resist, and for all my attempts to pretend it hadn't happened, we both knew I'd hurt her. I hadn't meant to, but it was Winterfest and we'd been drinking and laughing and the next thing I knew we were caught up in the moment.

I'd totally screwed up, and if she was coming back to perform, I was going to have to face it.

Dad jabbered on about the great town, and I was only half paying attention when he turned to me and said something about passing on his legacy. The crowd cheered.

Fucking fantastic. Not only did he plan out my life without my input, now he had the town in on it.

He passed the mic off to Grandma, who hugged him before stepping behind the podium. Honestly, Grandma was as bad as Dad in her self-importance. He'd had to learn it from somewhere, I guessed. She gave the history of Hale Bridge, working her way to the story's dark moment, when the Hale family had swept in to save the day.

"My late husband, Barnaby Hale, and I were honored to be of service to our community in the past, but this time the restoration of Hale Bridge is in your hands as well. The Hale Family Trust will match the collective contribution of this year's Winterfest proceeds, but we're going to need a significant amount of help funding this latest renovation. Especially so if the bridge is going to last to the end of our century and remain a standing monument in our town for our great-grandchildren and beyond."

With that, we were excused from our duties and I led the way off the steps and away from the expectant eyes of the town. The thing was, the idea of coming back here *someday* sounded pretty damn good to me. A home in Abbott Springs with a wife and a couple of kids—I could picture it. But I didn't want that life to be in the shadow of my father. I wanted more.

Looking up, I caught Aubree staring at me from behind a refreshment table and thought, *More.* She was helping Abbott's Sweet Confections pass out free cups of steaming hot apple cider. Her cheeks blazed pink in the winter chill, and she gave a soft half-smile before looking away.

I couldn't take my eyes off her. My brain kept playing that word on repeat as I looked at her. *More.*

Aubree

When I told my friends in Manhattan about Winterfest in Abbott Springs, they accused me of making it up. It almost defied description. Imagine that Frosty the Snowman devoured the town from *Gilmore Girls,* chased it with the Christmas-morning glee of a thousand giggling children, and then vomited it up in the middle of rural Ohio. That, my friends, was Winterfest.

Until the year I turned fifteen, Winterfest was my favorite weekend of the year. It surpassed Christmas—because I was that kid who already had everything. It surpassed my birthday—because despite what my friends might have thought, I didn't care for being the center of attention. Then Mom had made a promise she'd never intended to keep and an event that had once felt full of love and warmth left me lonely as shit.

But Mom was going to come—finally—and it just felt right. This was the year Winterfest would be good again.

"You see that?" Mrs. Hale pointed to Cynthia and Kennedy, who were at the top of the sledding hill where people were beginning to gather for the sledding races. "I think there's something going on between them. Now wouldn't they make the perfect couple?"

They were absolutely adorable together. Kennedy with his hometown, clean-cut, good-guy looks, and Cynthia with her classic blonde beauty. "She's just the kind of girl everyone would expect him to end up with," I replied. She wasn't right for Kennedy. He needed someone who would shake things up, keep him on his toes, and push him outside of his comfort zone. Someone who wouldn't ask him to live his days under his father's thumb in Abbott Springs.

Mrs. Hale narrowed her eyes, her brow furrowing as she frowned. "Hmm. I think you're onto something, Bree." I waited for her to explain what she meant but she didn't add anything further. Finally she shooed me forward. "Those sleds aren't going to race themselves."

"Oh, that's okay. I don't think I'm up for the sled races this year."

"Hey, Bree! Looking good!"

I turned to see Craig approaching us, his smile bright as he looked me over. Craig and Kennedy had played ball together in high school and gone on to play at different colleges. They were a little competitive, and Kennedy couldn't stand him. I didn't care for him much either, but he was mostly harmless.

"How's it going, Craig?"

He lifted a shoulder in a half-shrug. "It's good, but it'd be better if you'd be my partner in the boy-girl sled race."

"She'd love to!" Mrs. Hale said, winking at me.

I flicked my gaze to Kennedy, who was being pulled toward the sled shed by Cynthia. "Sure."

Craig's smile turned into an all-out grin.

When we reached the top of the sledding hill, Kennedy was standing way too close of Cynthia. Her laughter whirled through the air, and he tugged on the pigtails that were sticking out from underneath her wool hat. Pigtails. What was she? Six?

"It's good to have you back, Bree. This town isn't half as fun without you." Craig slung his arm around my shoulder and led me over to the old shed where people were pulling bright orange sleds into the snow.

Kennedy and Cynthia were heading out as we stepped up.

"Hey, man!" Craig said, extending his hand for Kennedy. They did one of those complicated guy fist-bump/high-five secret-handshake things. "Why'd you take off so soon last night? I thought we'd shut Juke's down together."

"I wasn't up for it." Kennedy shifted his gaze to me and then back to Craig. "You and Bree racing together?"

Craig pulled me in closer to his side. "Apparently it's my lucky day because I talked her into it. You two want to join us for drinks after? Loser buys?"

Normally, I would push Craig back a few feet and give him a lecture about personal space, but as juvenile as it was, I liked the jealousy I saw in Kennedy's eyes when he looked at us.

"We're up for that," Kennedy said, smirking at me. "Hope you brought your wallet, Picasso."

I ducked out from under Craig's arm to grab the last decent-looking sled. "Don't count on it."

They were calling all racers, and we hurried over to line up at the top of the hill. Craig and I climbed into our sled, me sitting between his spread legs, him wrapping his arms around me as our gloved fingers held the rope.

His chest was warm against my back, his breath in my ear.

Next to us, Cynthia wiggled her ass against Kennedy's crotch and giggled. I had to concentrate *really hard* on not calling her out on it.

"I should have asked you to do this years ago," Craig whispered in my ear. "Kennedy always keeps you close like he has some sort of claim to you. Everybody knows you two are fuck buddies, Bree. I'm just wondering when it's my turn."

What the fuck?

I turned, grasping for words more eloquent than "fuck off."

"On your mark," said a gray-haired man with an orange flag. "Get set!"

"See you at Juke's," Kennedy called, winking.

"Go!"

Then, someone gave our sled a push and we were off, flying down the hill alongside Kennedy and Cynthia, my heart pounding from adrenaline and anger.

The wind whipped around my face as we flew past a couple of other sleds and into the finish line, where Mrs. Hale stood clapping and cheering.

"It's a tie!" the line judge declared.

Craig grabbed my ass, and I jumped. When I turned, he winked at me. "Sorry. Couldn't help myself," he murmured. Then he stood and offered me his hand.

I grabbed it, caught him off-balance, and pulled him down into the snow. "Sorry," I said, standing on my own and stepping away from him. "Couldn't help myself."

Kennedy was glaring at Craig, his jaw hard.

"Kennedy and Bree," Mrs. Hale said, "can you go one more time? I have pictures of you two sledding down that hill together all through high school. I want a new one."

"We can just pose here," I suggested, but Kennedy was already tugging on my coat sleeve.

"Come on, Picasso. One more trip down the hill won't hurt you. It's tradition."

And just like that, I was heading back up the sledding hill, following a petulant Kennedy.

He didn't say a word to me. He positioned the sled for the next race and climbed in.

I crossed my arms and scowled until he gave me the courtesy of a little eye contact. "I'm not climbing into that sled with you if you're going to be grumpy."

He lifted a brow. "What? You afraid I'm going to snuggle you to death?"

More like I was afraid he wouldn't. To be in Kennedy's arms and have him do his damnedest not to touch me? I couldn't imagine much else that painful. "You could steer me into the lake or something."

"Get in, Picasso."

"I'll pass."

He threw up his hands. "I promise not to steer us into the lake. Come on."

"Racers on their marks!"

Kennedy reached over and grabbed my arm, tugging me into the sled with him. I collapsed between his legs and swallowed hard at the feel of his solid chest behind me. I grabbed the rope with both hands.

"I don't understand you," he whispered.

"On your marks!" the announcer called, and Kennedy slid his fingers over mine. He wasn't holding the rope so much as holding my hands. "Get set! Go!"

I'd been trying to keep some distance between our bodies, but my stick-straight posture couldn't hold against the momentum of our ride down the hill and my body sank into his. I closed my eyes to the whipping wind and concentrated on the feel of our bodies pressed together, the heat of his breath on my neck.

Too soon, the sled slowed and I opened my eyes to the chaos of the finish line.

"Got it!" Mrs. Hale announced, holding up her camera. "You two are adorable."

"We're a good team, aren't we?" Kennedy asked. Then he whispered, "Hold on," and was pushing off again. Trees blew by in a blur as we rushed down the wooded portion of the hill and Kennedy expertly steered our sled on a wild path through the trees. We picked up speed, faster and faster until the lake was in front of us and Kennedy had to pull up sharp to stop the sled.

We veered right and spun a one-eighty before the sled flipped and sank into the thick bed of snow, and Kennedy's body was on top of mine. He propped himself up on his elbows and grinned down at me.

"Where'd you learn to drive?" I shoved him off me and pushed out of the snow before I could register the feel of his body on top of mine. The weight of it as he looked down at me.

He hopped out of the snow and dusted off his pants. "There's excitement here, too, Bree."

"You're kidding me, right? A sled ride through the woods is supposed to convince me not to go to Paris?"

"No. Yes." He drew a hand through his hair. "I don't know. Just *think it through*, okay? You're so impulsive, and I don't want to see you get hurt."

I propped my hands on my hips. "Fine. I'll think it through if you do something impulsive."

"That doesn't even make sense."

I lifted my palms. "I don't want life to pass you by, Kennedy. Stop thinking and start living."

His gaze dropped to my mouth. I didn't so much step forward as gravitate toward him.

"I think they're down here somewhere."

I barely registered Craig's voice as I stared at Kennedy, daring him to touch me.

"There they are," Cynthia called.

Kennedy backed away from me, and my heart sank.

"Are we still getting those drinks?" Craig asked.

I swallowed and forced a smile, but my head was spinning with confusion. "I need to go home and take care of a few things. You guys have fun."

Kennedy—October

"Stop, please." I chased Kelsey down the stairwell and out into the cold, but I felt like most of my mind was still back in the room with Bree. *Naked* Bree.

Fuck. I really wasn't interested in chasing after Kelsey right now. I wanted to know what the hell Bree had been thinking. But this wasn't one of those times you just let your girlfriend steam for a few hours and get over it on her own.

"Kelsey! Stop. You're overreacting."

She spun on me, her eyes blazing. "There was a naked girl in your bed. I'm supposed to be cool with that?"

"She's a friend from back home."

"Is that supposed to make me feel *better*?"

I dragged a hand through my hair. What was Bree thinking? And why *had* she been naked? Because she was waiting for me? Hell, for all I knew she'd come to town, hooked up with one of my roommates, and fallen drunk into my bed. "I don't know what she was doing there, okay? I didn't know she was coming to town."

Kelsey's eyes glistened with tears and she sniffed. "I thought you were a nice guy, Kennedy. I thought I could count on you to not be an asshole like everyone else."

"What do you want me to say?"

Her teeth sank into her bottom lip as she studied me. "I want you to tell me that you aren't attracted to her. I want you to tell me that if we weren't together and you'd gone back to your room to find her tonight nothing would have happened."

"But we are together," I objected.

"I need to know that you would have sent her slutty, tattooed ass away, even if you didn't have a girlfriend."

"She was drunk, Kels. I don't fuck drunk girls." Even if the sight of the drunk girl in question had turned my whole body into a live wire.

She scoffed and lifted her chin to study the night sky. "You're so noble, aren't you?"

There was nothing I could say, so I shoved my hands in my pockets and waited as she fought some sort of internal battle. It took every fiber of my self control to stand here when I wanted to run back up to the room. Back to Bree.

"You'll cut it off with her?" Kelsey finally asked.

"What?" Okay, it made sense why she'd be confused. "No, Kelsey, Bree and I are not together. We never have been. She's an old friend. That's it."

"If we're going to stay together, I need you to break it off with her. Tell her you can't be her friend anymore. That's the only solution here."

Two weeks. Maybe two and a half. That was how long Kelsey and I had been dating exclusively. In what world were such demands acceptable after two weeks? "You want me to drop a lifelong friend because she got drunk and made a mistake?"

Her hand was soft as she reached up to stroke my cheek. "You're so sweet, Kennedy, but that was no mistake. She was there to seduce you, and she'll do it again. She doesn't even care that she's ruining your friendship, and she definitely doesn't care that she's threatening your relationship with me. So, yeah, it's her or me."

"You can't be serious."

"As a heart attack."

"She's been my friend since we were kids. She spent half of her high school nights staying in the room next to mine at my parents' house. I'm not just going to throw away our friendship."

She dropped her hand and backed up a step. "And yet she just proved how easily *she* was willing to throw it away. Goodbye, Kennedy."

I watched her go, the leaves crunching under her boots as she scurried up the steps to her dorm. I waited for the hurt and regret to hit, but it never came. Our relationship was too new to feel like a loss.

I jogged back up to my quad. My roommate Ted was watching TV in the common room when I came through the door. I blew past him and into my bedroom, but it was empty.

"She left," Ted called.

"Fuck!" I slammed my fist into the wall, and a sharp pain shot up my arm. I rubbed at the pain and squeezed my eyes shut. Leave it to Bree to pull something like that and run away.

When I looked up, Ted was leaning in the doorway. "No offense, man, but you chased down the wrong girl."

CHAPTER
Seven

Aubree

$\mathcal{I}$ was soaking in the tub at home when I heard the pounding of feet racing up the stairs. I sat up, water sloshing around me and my heart kick-starting as I reached for a towel. After Kennedy's almost kiss, I needed to be alone, but the sound of heavy steps in my empty house sent my mind back to the night I'd been here alone and those men had broken in.

"Come on, Bree! Where are you?"

The door swung open at the same moment I registered that it was Kennedy calling me.

He stepped into the bathroom, and I sank back into the bubbles, my hand pressed against my chest. "You scared the shit out of me," I grumbled, closing my eyes.

"Why did you just run off like that? Don't you think it's time we finish this conversation?" His gaze dropped to the bubbles and the blood drained from his face, as if he only just realized he'd walked in on my bath. His Adam's apple bobbed. "I'll wait in the bedroom."

Then he turned on his heel and walked out of the bathroom,

leaving me alone with the bubbles and my pounding heart.

So much for a relaxing bath to clear my head.

I pulled the drain on the tub and climbed out, drying my arms and legs and running the towel through my hair before wrapping it around my body and tucking it under my arms.

I didn't have any clothes in here, since I hadn't expected company, so I had no choice to face Kennedy in nothing but my towel for the second time in as many days.

When I stepped into my bedroom, he was sitting on the edge of my queen-sized bed, elbows resting on his knees. There was a bottle of whiskey dangling from his hand.

"I didn't mean to interrupt you," he mumbled. "Cynthia told me Craig made some comment about meeting you here and I thought—"

"You thought I was going to spread my legs for him just because he asked."

"No. I thought—" He dragged a hand through his hair. "I don't know what I thought. I'm sorry."

"You don't owe me an apology."

He pushed to standing. "Get dressed and come hang out with me."

"Always trying to get me to put more clothes on," I muttered. I turned to find my bag.

"What?"

Shit. I hadn't meant for him to actually hear me, but it was too late now. I lifted my chin. "You are the only guy I've met who's not related to me who wants me to put more clothes on."

"You're upset that I want you to get dressed before we drink and shoot the shit?"

I scoffed, rolling my eyes. "I'm not *upset* about anything. I'm merely making an observation."

"An observation about how you want me to look at your mostly naked body?"

I spun on my heel and stomped back to the bathroom, but he beat me to it and his hand stopped the door before I could slam it shut. I could only stare at him wide-eyed as he kicked the door wide and leaned against the frame.

I narrowed my eyes at him. "What are you doing?"

He took a slug of whiskey. "I care about you, Bree. And if asking you to put clothes on makes you feel bad, then I'm not going to do it. My mom taught me to consider the feelings of others."

"You know that's not what I meant. I'm not going to sit around in my towel while we drink."

"Then lose the towel."

I growled. Actually *growled,* I was so incensed. He had me cornered in the bathroom, with a nothing but a towel on, and I felt like the world's biggest fool. "Do you even know that I'm a girl? A woman? A female with working parts?"

"I can only assume the parade of men in and out of your life equates working parts."

"Whatever. I'm getting dressed."

He crossed his arms, eyes glued to me. "Whatever makes you comfortable."

I lifted my palms. "So leave?"

"Nah, you seem pretty convinced that I don't see you as a sexual creature. I think we'd both feel better if I watched that towel come off."

A hot flush rushed through me, all the way from my toes to the tops of my ears.

"You're blushing." His lips quirked, and I could almost make out that dimple. "I didn't even know you did that."

If he was going to play this game, I could give it as good as I got. "Have it your way then, Kennedy." I dropped the towel onto the floor and put on my biggest smile as I pushed past him. I could feel his eyes on me, and the silence in the room was palpable.

Settling the bag on the edge of the bed, I unzipped it and found a pair of yoga pants and a tank top. I didn't bother with underwear or a bra and took my time stepping into the pants and pulling the shirt over my head. Every movement felt heavy with significance, every second loaded with this ridiculous prayer that he was just about to spin me around and kiss me stupid.

Of course, he didn't.

I carefully arranged my face into a smirk of indifference, as if I'd just won this little power play, but on the inside I was just like my old dog Paws, lying on the deck, miserable and wondering if it was really worth it.

When I turned back, his eyes were on me—had he ever taken them off?—and his chest was rising and falling faster than normal. "You have new tattoos," he whispered.

I wanted to crawl under the covers. I had just stripped down to my birthday suit in front of Kennedy Hale, and all he was going to say about it was that I had new tattoos? "Do you object?" I grabbed the bottle of whiskey from his hand, our fingers brushing. If ever a moment called for liquid courage, this was it. "I still remember how annoyed you were when I got my first one."

"I wasn't annoyed."

I screwed off the top of the bottle and took a swig. "Yes, you were. You said, and I quote, 'How fucking stupid, Bree.'"

"I was jealous you were more of a badass than me. That new one is hot. Come here." Suddenly, his hands were on my hips and he dragged me in front of him.

"What are you—"

He stood behind me, his stance wide as he drew me between his thighs. Sliding his fingers into my waistband above my right hip, he turned me slightly and peeled the material down just far enough to expose my right ass cheek and my new infinity tattoo. He traced the symbol with his fingers. The gentle scrape of his calloused fingertips against my sensitive skin sent little shivers through me.

"Let me guess. You're jealous of that one too? I'll tat your ass for you, Kennedy. You just say the word." Just once I wanted to enjoy a moment without hiding behind my smart mouth, but I couldn't help it. Defense mechanism or whatever.

He traced the symbol once. Twice. By the third tortuously slow tracing, my legs were jelly. Then he took his hand away and released the waistband so it snapped back into place. My whole body cried out in protest.

"There was another one too," he whispered. His voice was

deeper, rougher. Was I imagining that? His hand slid up my tank, searching for the tattoo at the base of my spine. My nipples pebbled tight at his touch. "Let me see this one."

I swallowed. Hard. Then pulled my tank up and held it under my breasts, leaving my lower back and stomach exposed. I stood there between Kennedy's legs as he traced the vine at the base of my spine, following it around under my breasts. I wouldn't let myself think or hope. I couldn't. I wanted more too badly.

He took another step closer, all but eliminating the air between our bodies. I couldn't see him and didn't dare look, but his breath sent shivers through me as he lowered his mouth to my ear. "I don't do impulsive," he whispered, fanning his fingers over my belly. He pulled our bodies close together. "I do slow and methodical. I think about things."

His fingertip slipped under the waistband of my pants, and I gasped. "I think about things too."

"Did you think about sliding naked into my bed or was that an impulse?"

An electric buzz shivered its way down my spine. "I told you I was sorry."

"I never asked for an apology."

Kennedy

She'd dropped the towel. I'd baited her, and she'd taken it. I didn't think my heart would ever recover from that moment. Her ass had just enough jiggle to it, and even though she'd kept her back to me as she pulled on her clothes, I got a glimpse of her bare breasts. They were small—it was something she always joked about—but they were perfect. *She* was perfect.

For years, I had denied myself my feelings for Bree, but tonight I was done denying. Blame it on the whiskey. Blame it on the hurt in her eyes when she'd accused me of not noticing she was a woman. Blame it on the sexy tattoo on her ass that made my mouth water from wanting to bite it so badly.

She stood stock-still as once more I traced the vine up her spine and around her ribcage. I could see the goose bumps rising on her skin, and it was more instinct than seduction that had me leaning forward and blowing against her spine. Her body shuddered toward me, and just like that, my mouth was on her, her skin warm under my lips.

"Kennedy," she murmured.

I loved hearing my name on her lips. Bree saying my name, arousal making her breath come harder. I snaked my hand around the front of her body, following the path of the vine. She released her shirt and braced herself on the edge of the bed, bending slightly at her hips.

A groan slipped from my lips, and I nipped at the base of her spine.

I moved my hand slowly, wanting to memorize every inch of her soft skin. We were doing this. For better or worse, I was touching Bree, making her pant. The idea was equal parts exhilarating and terrifying.

I cupped her breasts and bit back a moan at how good they felt in my hands. Dipping my head, I opened my mouth against her shoulder blade, scraping my teeth over the bone, skimming my tongue over her tattoo. She leaned back, rolling her backside against my erection as I rolled her taut nipples between my fingers.

"You're so fucking sexy, Bree."

She spun in my arms and went to work on the buttons of my shirt. God, were her hands shaking? She pushed it from my shoulders and let it drop to the floor. "It's about time you noticed," she said, and when she looked up at me again, I saw it. The vulnerability in her eyes. The fear behind the bravado.

"You think I didn't notice?" I pulled my undershirt off over my head so I could feel her breasts against my bare chest. Then I pressed my mouth to hers because the fear in her eyes was breaking my heart and I wanted to wash it away. She opened under me, kissing me with the same impatient greed I felt for her. Her hands slid into my hair. I cupped her face in my hands, trying to slow this down, trying to take back control. She was trying to be the careless

seductress, but I wanted more than sex. I wanted in. I wanted…
Bree.

"You shouldn't have bothered with the clothes," I growled.

She whipped the tank off over her head before I could get to it. Then she pushed me back until I was sinking into the chair by her bed and she was straddling my hips. I wanted to break through her shell, but I was so damn hard, my erection pressing against my jeans, and she gasped as she settled against me.

Her lips parted slightly, she wrapped her arms around my neck. "What are we doing?" she moaned, rocking her hips against me.

"Being impulsive," I murmured.

"Kennedy." Then her lips were on me again, her body pressed close. My dick throbbed, aching with the tease in her movement. When she pulled back, her blue eyes had darkened and her lips were parted.

"You're so gorgeous."

She licked her lips and ran her gaze over my torso. "Likewise."

I liked this position. A perfect view of her breasts. Easy access to her mouth. But I needed access to more of her. I slid my hands under her ass, holding her as I stood. In two long strides, I was lowering her onto her bed.

She settled her hands above her head and grinned up at me. "Come here then."

"Not yet." I'd lose myself if I started touching her now. Fuck. If she moaned loudly enough, I'd probably even go off in my jeans. I wasn't willing for this moment to rush by. Not when I'd thought about it for so long.

I touched each of her tattoos, starting with the vine under her ribcage, then moving to the four-pointed star inked over her heart between her breasts. "Do you have any others?"

Her tongue darted out to wet her lips as she nodded. "The inside of my left foot."

I moved down the bed and lifted her foot. Right along the instep, a fine script said *Carry on.* "Fuck, Bree. Even your feet are sexy." I pressed a kiss there, and she giggled.

"Ticklish?"

She propped herself up on her elbows, giving me a fabulous fucking view of her breasts. "Little bit."

It seemed wrong that I didn't know that before. "Any others?"

"Ankle."

I pushed up her yoga pants to find a braid tattooed like an anklet on her skin. I stroked it, slid my hands up her pant leg, massaged her calf. "Where else?"

"Inner thigh," she whispered.

My breath left me in a rush. My eyes locked on hers. Her pupils were wide, turning her bright blue eyes dark. She lifted her hips off the bed, and I peeled the dark cotton off her legs.

And just that quickly, she was naked again. Twice in the span of twenty minutes because apparently I was the luckiest son of a bitch in the world.

I loved looking at naked Bree. I loved the way she just lay there unashamed, with her arms over her head as I ran my gaze over her, from her face and her eyes to her breasts, to the flat of her belly, then finally to the softness of her bare thighs.

"Let me see," I whispered, grazing her hipbones with my fingertips.

Her chest rose and fell as she slowly parted her thighs, exposing herself to me.

I climbed onto the bed and dropped to my elbows between her legs, my face so close to her sex it had my head spinning. The tattoo was a snowflake the size of a silver dollar, but its design wasn't the generic snowflake seen in winter decorations. The webbing was artful, intricate.

"Did you do design this?"

Her belly sank with her shaky exhale, and I traced the pattern. "Yeah."

"You're so talented." Then I removed my fingers and placed my open mouth against the design. She gasped. I parted her thighs farther and sucked on that sensitive spot until she whimpered.

"Kennedy. Please."

"Even some impulses shouldn't be rushed."

I trailed soft kisses over her body. I loved the dip in her collarbone, the soft, subtle swell of her breasts, and I tasted each, my tongue tracing the hills and valleys of her body, my mouth wrapping around the hardened peaks of her nipples. As I sucked, her back arched and her hands slid into my hair, tugging as she let out a soft little moan. It wasn't enough for me. I wanted to make her lose control. I wanted to make her cry out while her body shook under my touch.

I sucked harder at her breast and slid a hand between her legs.

She drew in a little gasp as my fingers connected with the slick, sensitive flesh between her legs. Better. Closer. I could feel her unraveling. But I still wanted more.

I pushed myself down, trailing my mouth across her stomach as I made my way between her legs. "I just can't get enough of this spot." I ran my fingers over the tattoo at her inner thigh then followed my touch with my mouth. I tasted her art with hot, open-mouthed kisses until I could feel the muscles in her thighs trembling under my mouth.

Then I parted her legs and set my mouth to the slick, wet folds of her sex.

She whimpered my name. God, I loved the breathy sound of it coming off her lips like that. Like she was wound tight, ready to come, and I was the only one who could get her there.

I investigated her with my tongue before sucking her clit into my mouth and listening to the sweet sound of her cry. Her fingers found my hair and tugged me up. I obeyed the wordless command, moving my body up the bed until I hovered over her.

Her kiss-swollen lips parted. Her cheeks flushed. I wanted to remember her like this. Her blue eyes softened as I looked down at her, the passion there weaved with tenderness that tore at something in my chest. I slid on a condom and settled over her again. She lifted her hips off the bed, rocking herself against my erection.

Her name left my lips and my breath left my lungs as I slid into her. Hot and tight and amazing. I tried to take it slow, to give her time, but she shifted under me and drew her legs around my waist, pulling me deep, draining my restraint.

I kept kissing her. I didn't want to stop kissing her. So as our bodies moved, our tongues met again and again, and I abused her lips with my greedy mouth until she gasped against me, close to coming.

Sliding my hand between our bodies, I found her clit and stroked it with my thumb until she squeezed me so tight I wasn't sure I could get her there before I lost control.

I drew back to watch her. "Come on, sweetheart. Let me feel you come." Then I pressed deep, and she pulsed hard and tight around me and pulled me into the abyss with her.

Aubree

Things I could have guessed correctly if they'd been on a test:

1. Kennedy Hale was a fucking spectacular lover.
2. His lovemaking made all the other douchebags I'd slept with look like fumbling idiots.
3. Now that I had him in bed with me, I never wanted to leave.

His eyes were half closed, his lips a breath from mine. I didn't ever want to leave this bed. I didn't want to go back to the real world where nothing was simple. I just wanted to sit here with Kennedy's scruff scratching my skin as he nuzzled the side of my neck.

I ran my hands over the muscles of his back. I wanted to paint this man. To sketch him with charcoal. To bring him to life with pastels. He was so gorgeous, and if I could capture him in my notebook, I could take my memories to Paris with me. I sighed.

The clock beside the bed read five-oh-nine, and if I wanted any hope of catching Everly's show in Cleveland, I needed to leave now.

"Come with me tomorrow," he murmured.

"What?"

His brow was furrowed, as if he was thinking about something difficult. "We're hosting a lunch for the board tomorrow. I want to tell them that I'm not coming home, that I'm going to take a chance with football."

I sat up. "Shut up."

"I'd rather not." He grinned at me. "I'm trying to have a serious conversation here."

"Kennedy..." My throat was thick, and the words didn't want to come out.

"Maybe you can teach me something about taking a risk."

"You totally just made my day."

He winced. "Seriously, you can't say that to a guy when the other part of your day was amazing sex."

Pushing him to his back, I straddled his hips and took his hands in each of mine. "Amazing, huh?"

He grinned, running hungry eyes over my bare breasts. "Fucking spectacular. I'm not too proud to admit that. What about you?"

I lifted a shoulder in a half shrug. "It was all right, I guess."

"You're killing me, Picasso." His hands went for my sides, tickling me until I doubled over with laughter.

"Slightly...better than...average," I managed between squeals.

His hands shifted from my sides to my ass and suddenly he was rolling us over so I was on my back and the delicious weight of his body was on top of mine. "In that case, I demand a rematch."

His kiss was firm and coaxing. As I parted my lips to taste him, he parted my thighs with one of his.

I was going to be late for Everly's performance.

CHAPTER
Eight

Aubree

Donuts downstairs for my junk food junkie. See you at the Pancake Breakfast. –K

Yawning, I set the note back onto the nightstand, where Kennedy had left it for me. I climbed out of bed and padded toward the shower.

I couldn't stop smiling as I washed my hair and shaved my legs. When I'd gotten back to Kennedy's house after the concert last night, the house was quiet. I climbed into his bed, and he was already there. He pulled my body against his before he set about seducing me with the slow movements of his deft hands and the heat of his mouth against my neck. We made love slowly and silently, our hands intertwined in the darkness.

I took my time getting ready, a smile returning to my lips every time I thought of him, but by the time I headed to Village Hall, I was practically jogging, so anxious to see him again.

From the lobby through the back door, Village Hall was usually bustling during the Pancake Breakfast, but the second I walked through the doors of the front entrance, I knew something was off. I could hear the clanking of dishes in the cafeteria beyond and smell bacon and maple syrup, but the typical chorus of gabbing friends was absent from the lobby.

Kennedy and his parents were standing over at the mural, contemplating it in silence. My gaze shifted from them to the chalk mural and my breath caught.

"They found it when they opened the hall this morning," Kennedy said softly. "We'll figure out who did it."

I felt arms come around me and smelled the cloying vanilla of Mrs. Hale's perfume. "I'm so sorry, sweetheart. It's so terrible."

Yellow police tape cordoned off the area in front of the defaced chalk mural. Mom's face barely recognizable with the B of "WANNABE" smudged across the portrait.

"Kennedy," Mrs. Hale said as she took her son's arm. "Take Bree into the cafeteria. Looking at this is just going to upset her."

I couldn't make my mouth form words to object. I wanted to tell her it didn't matter. I wasn't upset. But I'd grown up seeing my mom's face in Village Hall. The Hales were on one side of the lobby, my parents on the other, to commemorate the families who'd funded the community gathering place. Even when she'd left town, she'd still been here. But someone had wiped her out of my life here with nothing but the swipe of a finger.

Kennedy ushered me to a table in the cafeteria, and before I realized he'd left, he was returning with a mug of coffee. Everyone was staring at me, and the pity on their faces made me feel so ridiculous. It was a stupid chalk mural. This wasn't the first time it had been smudged; it was just the first time the damage had felt malicious.

"Drink." Kennedy nudged the mug toward me, and the scent of peppermint hit my nose. Friends would bring you a cup of coffee while you got your bearings. Real friends would spike said coffee with peppermint schnapps.

With a shaky smile, I took a healthy swallow, not even caring when the hot liquid scorched my tongue. Next he brought me two plates piled high with pancakes and bacon. He set a plate in front of me, and when I didn't touch it, he stabbed a piece of pancake with his fork and offered it to me. I took the bite obediently but shook my head when he offered a second.

We sat in silence for a minute, and I sipped at my coffee, waiting for the alcohol to hit my system, but there wasn't enough to give me a buzz, sadly.

"It was probably just some stupid kids, Bree. Don't let it get to you."

"I'm fine," I managed finally. "It's no big deal." But it was a big deal. When Mom came to town, she was going to see that and then she'd never want to come back. Why did her wanting to be here matter so much to me anyway?

I pushed my pancakes around on my plate, but my appetite from this morning had vanished completely.

"You can fix it, can't you?"

I snapped my head up so fast that I jerked my fork and a pancake went flying off my plate. "What?"

"Come on, Bree. You have more talent than anyone I've ever met. You can fix it."

I hadn't even thought of that. If I got it done today, would she find out about it when she arrived tonight? "Maybe," I whispered. "Yeah, maybe I could."

He grinned, and my heart did acrobatics in my chest just because that dimple was aimed at me. "That's my girl." He patted my hand and stood. "You can still make it to lunch today?" The vulnerability in his eyes made me forget the mural for a few beats. I was worried about some smudged chalk, and Kennedy was looking at a day where he was going to disappoint the hell out of his father.

"I'll be there, Kennedy."

"You're the best. I'll catch you in a few, okay?" He smiled and winked at me, but there was no kiss, no hug, no public display of our new relationship before he was walking away, heading toward his father and his duties as heir Hale.

"You want any more coffee?"

I looked away from Kennedy's retreating form to see Maya standing at my table a pot of coffee. "Yes, please."

"I'm sorry about the mural," she whispered. "I guess this will be the first year you'll be glad when your mom doesn't show up like she promised."

"She's coming this year," I defended. "She'll be here tonight. In time for the art exhibition."

The pity in Maya's eyes pissed me off. Why did everyone think they knew more about my mom than I did? She'd come this year because we were leaving for France together tomorrow.

"Sit down, Maya. You work too much."

She slid into the seat beside me and poured herself a cup of coffee. "So are you sticking around for the Winterfest toast on Sunday night?"

I snorted. "If there's gonna be toast, there'd better be bacon."

She rolled her eyes. "You know what I mean."

I grinned. "Nah, I can't make it this year."

"But it's tradition!"

I shifted uncomfortably and avoided her eyes. "I'm leaving for Paris with my mom in the morning."

"Paris? I guess you've been in New York almost six months. It was time for you to move again. You'll be back for Winterfest next year though, right?"

"Sure," I said, though I didn't know what to expect out of next year. "I'll be back and I'll make sure I stay through Sunday night next year."

Her face lit up and she wrapped her arms around me. "I'm so excited for you. I hope Paris is awesome."

Someone screeched, followed by the sound of crashing dishes.

Maya released me and stood. "Gotta get back to work."

She bounced off into the crowd, leaving me alone with my thoughts. No one but Kennedy had been surprised about my move. Not Everly, not Mrs. Hale, not Maya. Was it because Kennedy didn't know me as well as they did or because he understood me better?

My phone buzzed. Mom's face smiled back at me from the screen. I accepted the call.

"Good morning, Mom! Isn't it like six in the morning there?" Mom was on the West Coast this week and was so *not* a morning person.

"I haven't been to sleep yet, darling. I've had the most amazing night. Charles took me out on his yacht, and well, you probably don't want to know the details, but it's safe to say Mama's still got it."

"I didn't doubt it for a minute, Mom." I wrapped my hands around my coffee, holding my phone between my ear and my shoulder. "What time does your plane get in tonight?"

"Oh, see, sweetie, that's why I'm calling. I'm not going to be able to make it. Charles is having this party and all of these Hollywood people are coming. It will be my last hurrah before Paris."

"But…you promised." Worse than the fact that I sounded like a child when I said the words was that I felt like one. Time shifted, and I was a little girl again. In that breath, I wasn't an adult capable of making her own decisions and her own mistakes. I was eight years old and looking for Mom in the audience of my first dance recital. I was nine and sitting on the couch in my Halloween costume, watching the clock tick past ten as I waited for her to get home and take me trick-or-treating. I was fifteen and looking for her at my first Winterfest Art Show. Her promises were nothing.

"I'll make it up to you," she said. Her voice was so perky and full of excitement. She was never that excited to spend time with me. But I kept betting on her. "You're not mad, are you? I know my Bree. She's too cool to make a big deal of something like this."

My stomach contracted painfully. *I know my Bree.* But she didn't. She didn't know me at all. "Have fun at the party, Mom."

"We'll get you moved to Paris another time. Or better yet, go ahead without me. The apartment's ready, and I can meet you there in a few days, a week at the *most.*"

"Right, Mom. Okay." But Paris didn't feel like the glowing beacon of possibility anymore. It just felt like an empty shell of lonely disappointment. Like every other city in the world. But the alternative? Coming back to Ohio to stay? That scared me even more than moving overseas.

Kennedy

When I finally escaped Dad, I couldn't find Bree anywhere. Maya said she'd seen her leave Village Hall, but she wasn't at Juke's. She wasn't at the bakery. I jogged back to her house and used my key to let myself in. She wasn't in her room. I finally found her in the basement, studying a portrait of her parents under florescent lights and making notes on a pad of paper.

She looked gorgeous in those harsh lights. She'd stripped off her sweater and stood in jeans, boots that came to her knees, and a tank. One strap had slipped, and my hands itched to push the other one down to match.

"Why didn't you—" I cut myself off at the sound of her jaggedly drawn-in breath. In all the years I'd known Bree, I'd seen her cry only once. She was fifteen and she had a painting in the Winterfest Art Show. Her mom had promised to return before the winners were announced. We all knew the ending to that story. Her mom never showed. Not that year or any year after.

I'd been itching for a fight when she'd disappeared on me after breakfast and I'd had to run all around town to find her, but the loneliness on her face made all my anger and frustration fizzle away.

"What's wrong? What happened?"

She didn't look at me but kept her eyes trained on the portrait. "I'm making a list of the supplies I'll need to fix the mural. It shouldn't be too bad." She grimaced. "Not that there's any rush. Mom's not coming tonight. Probably not ever."

"I'm sorry." I wished I were surprised, damn it, but Aubree's mom always let her down. The surprise would have been if the woman had actually shown up tonight.

She swallowed and swiped at her cheeks. "It's no big. I should have listened to you and everyone else. It was silly to think this year would be any different. But with Paris…"

Here I was, overwhelmed with too much attention from my parents, and Bree had none of that. Her dad was always traveling on business, and her mother did nothing but let her down.

I used to think her lucky. She'd been able to live her life without them hovering all the time. But maybe I was the lucky one. At least my parents cared enough to hover.

I closed the space between us until I was standing over her, her sweet face tilted up to me. God, I wanted to kiss her again. I'd spent all morning thinking about those lips, looking for her in the crowd, thinking of sneaking away and taking her with me. When she disappeared after breakfast, I thought maybe she was having second thoughts about us, about what we'd done last night.

"It's okay to be angry with her, Bree."

"I know."

"Do you?"

"Of course. She's a little self-involved, but it's not like she's abusive or something. Lots of kids suffer much worse at the hands of their parents."

"True. That doesn't mean she doesn't deserve your anger."

She had this smudge of golden chalk on her cheek, and I wiped it away with my thumb. Her eyes fluttered shut at the touch.

"She doesn't," she murmured. "She gives me everything I need. She's going to buy me a place in Paris, for God's sake. I'm lucky."

"I'm not sure anyone has ever given you what you need." I dipped my head and pressed my lips to hers, relishing her soft sigh against my lips. "Tell me what I can do for you," I whispered against her lips. "Tell me what you want. It's yours."

A hiss escaped my lips as her hand slid into the waistband of my jeans. Before I realized what she had in mind, she was unbuttoning my pants and pushing them from my hips. She sank to her knees as she tugged them down, her lips parted and kiss-swollen, her eyes wide and smoky, her tongue darting out to wet her lip.

"Bree," I moaned. "Get your ass back up here."

"You asked what I wanted," she murmured. She took me into her hand and moved over me with one long, self-assured stroke. I staggered back against the wall at the feel of her hand on me, her breath so close it teased the head of my cock.

Then she was parting her lips and opening her mouth against

me. She took me in slowly, just the head at first, circling it with her tongue before moving deeper. Centimeter by deliciously painful centimeter, she took my shaft into her mouth. It was all I could do not to jut out my hips and push myself deeper. I pressed my palms against the wall, praying for self-control. Then in one long, slick movement, she was taking me deep in her mouth and I couldn't stop my hands from tangling in her hair.

I kept my eyes opened. I had to remember this. Bree on her knees before me, her lips swollen, sliding over me, her mouth hot as she sucked me deep.

"Stop, baby." I was too close.

She pulled back, replacing her mouth with her hand. "Let me finish," she whispered.

I growled. Pulling her up, I took her mouth and seduced her with my lips. My body throbbed—I was so close—but I wanted to be inside her when I came. Slowly, I removed her tank then slipped her jeans from her hips. After grabbing the condom from my jeans, I led her to the couch and pulled her onto my lap.

I kissed her slowly, and when she pressed close and tried to change my tempo, I didn't waver. When her hands moved against the hot skin of my abdomen, I held steady.

She tasted like hot cocoa and felt like heaven. She was the warmth on the cold day, the sunshine breaking through the gloom. And I didn't know how to be any of that for her. So I kissed her until she was breathless and open. I kissed her until she stopped *trying* and started *being*. Until she softened beneath me, as open and vulnerable as this ache in my chest made me feel.

Then I shifted my hips and she settled onto me. I took her gasps, her pleas, and her sighs, and I held tight as she moved over me. I never wanted to let go.

CHAPTER
Nine

Kennedy

"How long have you and your girl here been an item, Kennedy?" George, the vice president of my father's company, took a giant bite of his sandwich as if he hadn't just sent my meal from uncomfortable to extremely awkward.

We were all gathered around my parents' oversized dining room table—Mom and Dad, my sisters, the board of Hale Construction, Aubree, and me.

"Um, we're not—" Crap. We hadn't had this discussion. Were we an item? Or was this just a weekend of no-strings sex? I'd pulled an Aubree and acted before I thought it through, and now look where I was.

"If I could have everyone's attention." My father pushed out of his chair, and all eyes turned to him. "George and I have an exciting announcement."

George Stevens stood up and grinned. Or I thought he was grinning. It was hard to tell behind all his facial hair. "As you all know," George said, "I've been anxious to retire for some time now, but I've been putting it off until we could find a suitable replacement. I have no doubt my wife shares my enthusiasm when I say that we've found that replacement and I will be transitioning into retirement between now and this summer."

I took a drink of my water and tried to be patient while I waited to return to my conversation with Bree. I hadn't wanted to get dressed and come play nice with the board. I'd wanted to spend the day with Bree. Alone. Naked.

"Kennedy, would you mind standing, son?" George extended a hand in my direction. "I'm pleased to introduce you all to the next vice president of Hale Construction."

Just like that, water was racing to my lungs. I coughed as my dad's chest puffed with pride.

"Kennedy will move back to Abbott Springs when he graduates in May and step right into George's position as vice president. We're all very excited."

Fuck me.

Everyone around the table started clapping, but I was still trying to cough the water from my lungs. George came around the table and slapped my back in a manly hug. "You'll do great, son."

My father was right behind him, wrapping his arm around me and smiling across the table. Another board member pointed his cell phone camera in our direction. "I wanted it to be a surprise, but your mother thought I should tell you."

Mother sent an aggravated glare at my father then gave me an apologetic smile. I'd bet my mother thought he should have told me before today—or hell, *ask* if I even wanted the position. But my father didn't get permission. He did as he pleased, everyone else be damned.

"I'm not sure this is what I want right now," I said. My father scowled, so I added, "*Sir.*"

"Nonsense," my father said. Then he returned to his seat like this conversation was over. "You're a Hale. This is in your blood."

My chest burned as I lowered back into my seat.

He was right. I was a Hale. I'd been working for my father's company my whole life. I'd be comfortable stepping into George's position. I'd be good at it. It was the sure bet.

"Actually," Bree began, and I squeezed her thigh under the table and shook my head. Now wasn't the time. She narrowed her eyes at me. "What if Kennedy—"

"Thank you, everyone, for all of your support," I said, cutting her off again. "It means a lot."

"You're a lucky man, son," my father said, turning his attention back to his plate. "We arranged this all for you."

He wasn't doing it for me. He was doing it for him. And if I wanted to live my own life for once? If I wanted to take a chance? Just to see what that was like? I should know better. I was a Hale, and that was asking too much.

My father and turned the conversation to Winterfest, and Bree scowled at me. She wanted me to tell them the truth, to tell them I wanted to go pro, but I would look like a complete fool if I did that now. She had no idea what it was like to be me. The people in this town loved her no matter what. But I had to earn it by living my life exactly as they deemed suitable.

When the meal ended, Bree calmly placed her napkin on her plate, hugged my mom, and left the house without a word to me.

"Go after her," Mom said, coming to my side.

"What?"

"Bree," she said. "She's obviously upset." She squeezed my shoulder and nodded toward the door. "There are a few hours yet before the parade. Go."

Aubree

"What are you doing?"

I looked up from my suitcase to see Kennedy walking into my bedroom. "I'm packing. I figure I'll be busy all night, so I need to get it done now."

His jaw ticked. "Why are you packing?"

Something flipped in my stomach. Guilt? Fear? Hope? I didn't even know. "My plane leaves in the morning."

"Your plane?"

I grabbed a pair of jeans from the pile of laundry on the floor. I hated goodbyes and I had no desire to have this conversation after our lovemaking had left me so emotionally raw. I folded the jeans carefully before settling them into the suitcase.

"You're actually going to do it. You're going to leave to be with her when only a couple of hours ago she let you down again."

I scooped up a sweater and kept my eyes trained on the soft knit as I folded. Anywhere but on Kennedy.

He crossed the room then flipped my suitcase shut before lowering to the edge of the bed, elbows on his knees, his face in his hands.

"When I want someone in my life, I'm willing to take a chance on them." Something crushed in my chest as I whispered the words.

"You take chances on all the wrong people," he growled, scrubbing his hands over his face. "You're going to spend your entire life being disappointed because you set people up to fail you. Your mom isn't going to be any better of a mother in Paris than she was in the States." He smacked his hands against his thighs and pushed himself back to standing. "The guys you follow across the country are just as big of losers on the East coast as the West. Quit giving everything to the people who are only going to let you down."

And what about him? Had he been one of the wrong people? I couldn't stop thinking about the look on his face when that man had asked if we were an item. Like he'd been caught shoplifting. "I'd rather be hurt again and again than let life pass me by because I'm playing it safe."

Slowly, he lifted his head, his blue eyes burning as he stared at me. "You think leaving makes you brave? Try something truly brave, Bree. Try *staying*. When shit gets tough and people don't live up to your expectations, try sticking around. You're not courageous. You're running away."

"Fuck you, Kennedy. At least I'm not allowing someone else to rule my life."

He picked up my purse from where I'd thrown it in the corner. My hands shook as I reached to take it from him, but he held tight.

"It's not the same. We both know football is just a dream. I'll have a good life here. You could too."

My eyes burned and I felt like I was looking at him through a fog. "What are you asking me?" I counted the beats of my heart pounding in my ears. *Thump. Thump. Thump.*

"I don't know what you want from me. This is just happening too fast. I need to time think. Space. I don't know. I can't just—"

The thumping stopped and for a second I couldn't breathe. "No, right. Of course you can't."

His shoulders fell and his fingers loosened their hold on my purse, and I took it and one last look at him. Then I ran.

Kennedy

Whiskey was good. Whiskey was way fucking better than waving at the crowd at some stupid parade. And it was better than thinking about Bree leaving. Bree asking me for something I didn't know how to give her.

I slugged back what remained in my glass and tapped it.

Juke frowned from behind the bar. "Don't you have a parade to get to?"

"Nah. I'm not gonna go this year."

Juke raised a brow but didn't say anything. He silently refilled my whiskey and left me to stew.

I must have lost track of time, but before long I felt a heavy hand squeezing my shoulder.

"Do you have any idea what time it is?"

I blinked up at my dad, whose cold-pinkened face was drawn into tight, furious lines. "Five o'clock somewhere," I said, lifting my glass. "Want a drink?"

His eyes blazed with anger, and I almost laughed. I never realized how his cheeks blazed when he was angry. He looked like a clown. "It's after six. You missed the whole parade. It started late because we were waiting for *you*. Why? So you could get drunk? Have you forgotten where your priorities are?"

Sliding off the barstool, I stumbled back a few steps before I got my feet under me. "I have no idea what *my* priorities are. I've never been allowed to have my own priorities. Only yours."

"Stop," he hissed. "You're acting like a spoiled brat."

I threw up my palms. "Maybe I am."

I could feel Dad's anger coming at me like a gust of wind as I pushed out of the bar. I heard him calling but his voice faded when the door settled behind me.

For the first time in my life, I didn't care what my dad thought. Maybe it was the booze talking, but I *wanted* to disappoint him. I wanted him to be angry with me. Maybe then he wouldn't want me around. Maybe I wouldn't have to do everything his way.

If it was after six, that meant the party at the old barn would be starting soon. Bree would be there. She wouldn't miss a performance by her precious Everly.

Hell, maybe I should have Everly ask her to stay. She had no problem leaving me behind, but she'd do anything for Ev. I neared the barn and spotted Everly and Justin Cohen.

"Speak of the Devil," I muttered.

Everly. Now there was a prime example of how much everything got screwed up when I broke the rules. Bree wanted me to take a chance, but I'd taken a chance on Everly, hadn't I? I'd liked her, and last year we'd slept together, but then Craig had made crude comments at the bonfire and she'd assumed I'd told the asshole. I hadn't had a chance to explain before she'd turned cold on me. Hated my guts for something I'd thought she'd wanted as much as I had. I never would have touched her if I'd have known. It hadn't been worth it.

Then I'd made the same fucking mistake with Bree. Only… Bree was Bree, and the memory of kissing her, touching her, sliding into her? I couldn't even make myself regret it.

"Seriously—I'm a big girl," Everly was saying to Cohen. "I can handle myself."

"You can say that again," I called. She could teach Bree a thing or two about handling herself. Everly might have hated me after we'd had sex, but she hadn't run away to goddamn Paris.

"Okay, I will," Everly was saying, but my mind was stuck on Bree, and I wasn't sure what she was talking about. "I'm a big girl," she repeated. "I can handle myself."

Cohen glared at me and clenched his fists. What was that about?

"Long time no see, Pinky." I touched the pink strand of her hair. She used to have a whole head of that pink hair, but now she just had the few streaks in the front. It reminded me of Bree's ever-present red streak, but it didn't do the things to my gut touching Bree's hair did. Why was that? Why couldn't we choose who we loved?

"Shame. I've missed you terribly," Everly said. Bitterness dripped off her words.

I never meant for things to get like this between us. I had to make this right. "Meet me at the lake later?"

"Pass," she hissed, and I winced as I realized what she must have thought I'd meant.

Cohen stepped in front of her before I could reply, totally cutting me off. "We gotta get going if we're going to run by your house."

"You're right," Everly said. "We should go. Great seeing you, Ken."

They started walking away, and it clicked. Cohen and Everly were together. Any other night, I wouldn't have cared. Fuck, I would have been happy for them even, but tonight it just pissed me off. Because I didn't want to be the only miserable SOB in this town. "Oh, it's like that with you two now?"

Cohen froze. "What the fuck is that supposed to mean?" He spun on me. Eyes blazing.

I held up my hands. "Hey, man. It's cool. Just be warned, she's a screamer."

The moment the words left my mouth, I saw Bree out of the corner of my eye, her mouth agape at my crudeness, hurt carved into her features.

And because I was so busy looking at Bree, by the time I saw Cohen's fist coming at me, I was already on the ground.

Aubree

Everly looked gorgeous tonight in her black cocktail dress and heels, and for the first time in my life, I resented her for being more beautiful than me. Even though I was the one who'd talked her into performing here tonight, I resented that she was brave enough to actually do it. To face her fear of performing at home and prove to everyone how good she was.

My chest ached. Kennedy had gotten in a fight tonight. Over Everly. Okay, I wasn't sure it was fair to call his face meeting Jubby's single right hook a "fight," but it definitely wasn't in character for Golden Boy Extraordinaire.

"Kennedy," Mrs. Hale said. "Why don't you dance? Bree, you'd dance with him, wouldn't you?"

"Come on, Picasso. We need to dance. It's tradition." He took me to the dance floor and draped my arms behind his neck. "Would you quit looking at me like you want to cut off my balls?"

There wasn't enough room in my chest for air when he was this close. He didn't even understand that he'd hurt me earlier. That had hurt even worse than his unwillingness to take a chance on me, so I made this about Everly when it should have been about me. "She's a screamer? Seriously, Kennedy? Who says that?"

Kennedy leaned his head back and looked at the beams spanning the width of the barn. They'd been wrapped in twinkling white lights for the dance. "I was referring to the way she fights."

Ducking from under his arms, I stepped back. "Whatever. Go give the honor of your company to one of your groupies. I'm not interested."

I left the barn, walked away from Everly's band and this feeling in my gut that I wasn't enough for Kennedy.

Worse was that I couldn't talk to anyone about it. If I told Everly, she'd spout venom about how much she loathed Kennedy for sleeping with her last year. If I told Maya or Sami, they would stress the fact that Kennedy needed time to process everything, that I should be glad he wanted to be in Abbott Springs. They wouldn't understand I was terrified I would give him that time, only to find I didn't measure up. That I wasn't enough for him. Just look at my mom. She'd given up a promising career when she'd gotten pregnant with me, and she'd spent every minute since she'd skipped town trying and failing to get that life back.

I wandered around town until my fingers and toes were numb and my thoughts had made a mess of my stomach. Like I always did when I felt lost, I went for my art supplies.

Kennedy

"Thought maybe you stood me up." A bitter breeze blew off the lake, stinging my cheeks as Everly joined me on the dock.

"Got held up."

I was so glad she was here. I didn't know what the hell I was going to do about Bree, but I did know I couldn't do anything until this thing between me and Everly had been resolved once and for all. "So, Pink. I get the distinct feeling you hate my guts. And I feel bad about the way things went down."

"Me too," she whispered. "I messed up."

That seemed like a bit of an overreaction. It hadn't been anything serious. "It's not like you killed anybody, Everly. Jesus. It was a hook-up. I thought you were fun to hang with. I was kind of in a weird place and didn't really know you had, like… expectations."

She closed her eyes and shook her head. "I think that was my problem, you know? I didn't even know what I wanted or expected from you. And then it felt like you'd used me for sex."

I winced. I never would have touched her if I'd known she'd react that way. "Ouch. I seem like that big of a dick, huh?"

She waited a beat before replying. "No. But it was my first time and—"

"What?" *What. The. Fuck.* My stomach churned, and it felt like all the whiskey I'd ingested earlier sloshed violently in my empty stomach. "Why didn't you tell—"

"Shh. Relax. I'm over it." She waved a hand dismissively, and it seemed like she actually meant what she was saying. "I think I thought it would prove something to people in this town if we were together. Like I was worthy of their respect or something. Sounds pretty dumb saying it out loud."

"Wow, now *I* feel cheap and used." I nudged her. She laughed and I relaxed a little.

"I've been carrying this stupid feeling of inadequacy around like a security blanket. It didn't work out with you, so why bother with anyone else?"

"That doesn't sound like the Everly Abbott I know." And it just proved what an epic fuck-up one impulsive night could cause.

"Right?"

"Naw, don't beat yourself up. We all do that to some extent, I think. Use our past failures as excuses for not taking a chance on the future." Jesus. Was that what I was doing? Using my screw-up with Everly to justify not moving forward with Bree? As if the situations were remotely similar. But my relationship with Bree was nothing like my relationship with Everly. And my mistake with Everly had been the sex. But having sex with Bree hadn't been a mistake. The mistake had been letting her go.

"How do we stop?" she asked.

"No idea." I wasn't just blowing her off. It was true. Even as I stood here knowing I needed to do something, I had no idea *what*.

"Well, what good are you?" She smacked my arm playfully.

I sighed. "Not much good to anyone. I'm pretty much a giant jackass, screwing up like it's my job lately."

"Join the club. My best friend decided to tell me he had feelings for me tonight. And I'm standing here with you."

"Ah, Cohen finally fessed up." I stopped walking and fingered my sore jaw. "Well, that explains why he was hell-bent on kicking my ass today."

"Yeah. Sorry about that."

"Sorry about the shitty remark. I haven't exactly had the best year ever. But that was disrespectful as shit and I didn't mean it."

"Hey, Ken?"

"Yeah?"

"You think maybe we get do-overs in life? Like sometimes we get to make mistakes, pick the wrong major, the wrong job, sleep with the wrong person even, and it's okay? Could it be possible that every little misstep isn't the end of the world after all?"

Bree appeared at the end of the path and gave a little wave but didn't come closer.

"Hope so," I murmured, watching Bree walk away. *I really hope so.*

Aubree

Two spotlights illuminated the mural as I touched up the portrait of my parents. I blended whites and yellows until I matched the almost-golden color of Mom's hair. Then I went about touching up the soft curl that fell over her cheek.

"I never realized how much she looks like you," someone said behind me.

Everly stepped into the light of my little workspace, her cheeks flushed from the cold as she frowned at the mural.

"The resemblance is startling, really," she said. "You could practically be painting a self-portrait."

I cut my eyes to her rosy cheeks. When Kennedy had slept with her, I'd been a little shocked and hurt, but I'd convinced myself that he'd been such an idiot about the whole thing because of his feelings for me. I should have been crowned Queen of Delusion. "I'm sorry Kennedy was such an ass tonight."

Everly shrugged. "I think we worked it out."

I'd seen them down by the lake. My heart wrenched at the image, but I pushed it away. I had no hold on Kennedy Hale. "You're not angry with him anymore?"

"I'm not. But I am a little angry with you."

I froze and put my chalk down before turning to her. "Why?"

"I've been bitching about Kennedy for all these months, and you had a thing for him all this time, didn't you?"

I busied myself organizing the chalk at my little workstation so I didn't have to answer.

"And you didn't tell me because I was so hung up on what happened. I'm sorry. I didn't know."

Something ached in my chest as I tried to imagine missing her shows when I moved to Paris. Everly was one of those friends whom I felt close to regardless of geography, and I knew that wouldn't change. She'd still be there for me. But I'd miss out on so much, and for what?

"It looks amazing," she said softly, stepping forward to study my work. "If I hadn't seen it for myself, I wouldn't believe someone had vandalized it."

"I should have left it. It's not like she's ever coming back to see it." I shrugged and forced a smile. "Kennedy wants me to be angry with her, but it's not like she'd notice if I was. I could kick and scream like a child, but I'd only be hurting myself."

Everly fingered my selection of chalk colors. "You're right. She'll probably never see it." She slid a red piece from its container and offered it to me. "I'm not sure she should be commemorated on an Abbott Springs mural."

My mouth gaped. I'd just spent hours correcting the image, and now Everly was suggesting— "I'd be as bad as the vandals."

"Vandals destroy. You, Aubree Baxter, create and inspire." She extended the brush to me and waited. "You've always inspired me. Hell, we wouldn't have had half the good times we did in high school if it weren't for you."

Slowly, I took it from her hands and studied the mural. Mom did look so much like me. Then I got to work.

CHAPTER
Ten

Kennedy

For the last day of Winterfest, the family met the board at Village Hall for what Bree and I called "The B&B"—breakfast and bullshitting. Part of me hoped I'd have an excuse to skip it this morning, that I'd be too busy making up with Bree, touching Bree, making love to Bree.

She didn't come home last night. Not to my home at least. When I'd sent her a text this morning, she didn't reply. Would she stop by Village Hall before she left for the airport? Or would she leave the country without saying goodbye?

"Kennedy!" my father called as I approached the hall. "Come over here! I want you to meet the newest city council members! Harvey, Grant, this is my son."

They were gathered on the sidewalk in front of the hall. I gave a polite smile and offered my hand to the two men. "It's nice to meet you."

We followed Dad inside, but my steps stuttered the second I walked in the door. Bree had fixed the mural, and it looked beautiful. Only, she'd altered it just enough so that it was no longer a portrait of her parents. If there was any doubt in my mind, the red lock of hair hanging in the woman's eyes made it clear. This was now a portrait of Bree and her father.

"You might as well get used to talking to Kennedy here," my father was saying. "In a couple of election cycles, he'll be the one making the run for mayor of Abbott Springs."

I couldn't take my eyes off the blue eyes staring back at me from the mural. Bree was right. I wasn't living my life as my own, and only because I was too scared to take a chance. Some things you needed to have faith in. Sometimes you needed to leap without looking.

"That's wonderful," Harvey said.

"Carrying on a legacy," Grant chimed in.

"Actually—"

"We just have to show him the ropes and let him know how this town runs," my dad said. "Then in maybe thirty years, he'll be preparing his son to run for office."

"No." I barked the word and I didn't know if it shocked me or my father more.

Harvey forced an awkward laugh. "Oh, he's not ready to think about children just yet."

"Take your time," Grant said. "Trust me. Nothing's better than those days as a single young man."

"No," I repeated, gentler this time. "I appreciate your faith in me, but I'm not going to be coming back to Abbott Springs after graduation. I won't be taking the position as vice president of Hale Construction, Dad, and I'm not interested in being mayor. Not right now at least. Maybe when I'm much older, but I need to live my own life first."

My father forced a laugh. "We'll talk about this another time, son."

"I'm sorry, sir. I don't want to disappoint you, but this isn't what I want for my life. I love football and I want to give a career as a pro a try."

My father sputtered. "But you're not even a draft prospect."

"No one at Waskeegee Tech is a draft prospect. And I might

fail," I said with a shrug. "Or maybe I can work my ass off and earn a chance at my dream."

"That's amazing, Kennedy," Harvey said. "You're a talented young man. I had no idea you were interested in pursuing professional football. I'm pleased to hear this."

Grant clapped his hands together. "An Abbott Springs native playing in the NFL. I like the sound of that."

My father's jaw was tight and I could see the frustration in his eyes. "Pipe dreams are a waste of time. Kennedy's just feeling idealistic after a weekend with his friends. We have a legacy."

I tucked my hands in my pockets. I thought this would be the hardest thing I'd ever done, but instead of feeling weighed down by my confession, I felt weightless. "This is something I have to do."

"Grant, Harvey, excuse me while I talk to my son?"

"I'm sorry, Dad. I can't talk now. I have a plane to catch."

"A plane?"

I nodded. "I can't let the girl I love move to Paris without telling her how I feel." When I turned to the door, Mom was staring at me with wide eyes.

She grabbed me into a hug. "I'm proud of you," she whispered. "You go after that life you want, Kennedy."

I squeezed her hard in return. "Thanks, Mom."

"Get Bree and bring her back here. You know as well as I do that she doesn't want to be in Paris."

"I know," I said softly, swallowing.

"Does she love you too?"

I shrugged. "I don't know, Mom. But I'd rather take the risk and fail than never have a chance with her."

She wiped a tear from her cheek and nodded. "Tell me if you need anything."

After another hug, I ran back to the house, snow crunching under my feet the whole way. I wouldn't make it to the airport in time to catch her plane but I would be right behind her. I'd find her in Paris and I would tell her how I felt.

My chest burned at the thought of what she might say, all the reasons she might turn me down. Again. But it was a risk worth taking.

When I got home, I took the stairs two at a time to my bedroom, but when I stepped in, I froze. Bree was sitting on the edge of my bed in a gray sweater and jeans that hugged her long legs, her hands folded in her lap, and I was so damn happy to see her. I just wanted to draw her into my arms and throw all my fear and longing and hope into kissing her. The moment I unfroze and took a step forward, she put up her hand to stop me.

"Back in October," she began, and my heart sank, "I should have done it like this. I should have come to you and told you how I felt. I never should have expected you to be ready to leap when you didn't even know there was a reason to try."

"No, I shouldn't have—"

She put up her hand again. "This is hard for me, Kennedy. Please let me finish?"

My chest sagged as I exhaled. "Okay."

"You're right about me. I take chances on people who are going to let me down. I set myself up for failure again and again. Because what if I take a chance on someone who can be trusted and even they let me down? At that point, I have to acknowledge that it's not them. It's me. I sabotage life by betting on the wrong things. I know that. But you have to understand that being let down by the wrong people is less painful than being let down by the right ones."

I sat next to her on the bed and took her hand, but I stayed quiet. She needed to do this.

"I couldn't bring myself to take a chance on you because since my mom moved away, you've been the best part of my life. I was afraid that if I told you how I felt—if I did it the *right* way—you'd reject me."

"So you did it the wrong way," I said quietly.

She nodded. "Impulsiveness is a scapegoat. If I hadn't shown up naked in your bed. If I'd just told you that I've been in love with you since I was fifteen. If I'd told you that no matter where I've lived, my relationship with you has been the best part of my life. If I told you that the only place I've ever felt safe was in your arms. If I'd said all that and you'd still turned me down…"

Her eyes filled, and I couldn't handle it anymore. I cupped her face in my hands and kissed her.

Aubree

One second I was spilling my heart onto the floor, and the next, he was kissing me.

He pressed his mouth against mine as his hand cupped my jaw, and I just sat there stupidly. Not pushing him away but too scared to kiss him back. Slowly he shifted our bodies so he was lowering me onto the bed. He parted my thighs with one of his.

Then he whispered my name against my lips and suddenly the fantasy was real. Hands in his hair, I slipped my tongue into his mouth and tasted him. He tasted like hot coffee and smelled like the boy I loved.

"I feel like I've spent half my life talking myself out of kissing you," he whispered.

I pushed onto my elbows and narrowed my eyes at him. "You could have fooled me."

He grinned and that little dimple appeared. If he hadn't already turned every bone in my body to goo, that dimple would have made my knees weak. "I was a teenage boy with a sexy chick sleeping on the other side of his bedroom wall. If you knew how many fantasies your proximity fueled, you'd file a restraining order."

I bit my lip. It was stupid how much I wanted to hear that. Needed to.

"Then sometimes you'd crawl into bed with me, and all I could do was hold you when I wanted to do so much more."

"You could have done more," I whispered, settling back onto his pillow. "I wouldn't have crawled in if I hadn't wanted you to."

"I needed you too much, Bree. You're the only one who ever really understood me, and I wasn't going to lose that." His Adam's apple bobbed as he swallowed. "I'm still afraid of losing that, and I panicked yesterday. But today I told Dad and two city council members I was going to try for the NFL."

"Kennedy." Something squeezed in my chest. "I know you can do this."

He shrugged. "Maybe. Or maybe I'll fall on my ass. But this wise chick I know was right. I have to try now." He smoothed his thumb over my cheek. "Some decisions don't need to be analyzed. They're just right. I love you, Aubree Baxter. Don't leave me."

"I'm not going anywhere." As quickly as the words slipped from my lips, his mouth returned to mine. I loved the taste of him, the weight of his body on mine, the feel of his heat against my skin.

When he broke the kiss, he nuzzled my neck, his beard scraping the tender skin there. "You almost left too soon again," he murmured against my neck.

"Again?" I asked, my mind fuzzy from his kiss and the feel of his body on mine.

"You left too soon back in October. If we could have talked… I've always wanted you, Bree. More than anyone."

Now it was my turn to kiss him.

One kiss turned into another, and his hands in my hair became his hands under my shirt, and before long it was hours later and we were naked in his bedroom, holding each other as we listened to his parents argue downstairs.

"You never asked him what he wanted," his mom was saying.

"Of course I did." His father's voice boomed through the house. "Why would I do all this if he didn't want it?"

"Because *you* want it," his mom said. "You ever stop to listen to your daughter Gracie when she talks about wanting to be mayor? Or Joy when she talks about working for the company? Your son isn't the beginning and end of your legacy."

"Gracie wants to be mayor?" I asked Kennedy.

He shrugged and pulled me closer, the inch of air that had come between us apparently too much. "She'd be good at it. Bossy little shit."

I grinned then sighed into his touch.

My phone buzzed on his nightstand, and Kennedy grabbed it before I could.

"It's a text from Maya," he said. "It says, 'Hope you had a nice flight. We'll miss you at the bridge tonight.' Should I tell her you're not moving to Paris?"

"Hmm, I guess we should get dressed and go. We can tell them then." I climbed out of bed and grabbed my clothes. When Kennedy groaned in protest instead of following, I added, "Come on, sexy. I'll buy you dinner at Juke's after we go to the bridge."

"And after that?" he asked, skimming his eyes over me as he sat up in bed.

"Oh, I think I'll just keep you on your toes," I whispered. "Not everything needs to be planned."

He grabbed me around the waist and drew me forward, pressing his open mouth against my belly. "As long as it involves you, it's plan enough."

The End

ABOUT

LEXI RYAN

A *New York Times* and *USA Today* bestselling romance author, Lexi Ryan considers herself the luckiest chick she knows. Her books have been described as intense, emotional, and wickedly sexy. Lexi herself has only been described using two of those adjectives (feel free to guess but she's not telling). When not writing, she enjoys watching football, perfecting her chocolate martini, and reading her way to the title of Biggest Romance Fangirl Evah. A former college professor, her biggest fears include faculty meetings and large stacks of ungraded freshman composition papers. She now writes full-time from her home in Indiana, where she lives with her husband and two children and their neurotic dog. You can visit Lexi at her website www.lexiryan.com or find her on Twitter @writerlexiryan or Facebook at facebook.com/lexiryanauthor.

Other Titles by

LEXI RYAN

New Hope Series
Unbreak Me
Stolen Wishes: A Wish I May Prequel Novella
Wish I May

The Here and Now Series (A New Hope Series)
Lost in Me
Fall to You
All for This

Hot Contemporary Romance
Text Appeal
Accidental Sex Goddess

Stiletto Girls Novels
Stilettos, Inc.
Flirting with Fate

Decadence Creek Stories and Novellas
Just One Night
Just the Way You Are

This paperback interior was designed and formatted by

www.emtippettsbookdesigns.com

Artisan interiors for discerning authors and publishers.

www.ingramcontent.com/pod-product-compliance
Lightning Source LLC
Chambersburg PA
CBHW070639130626
46555CB00006B/2614